Alice Brown

By Oak and Thorn

A Record of English Days

Alice Brown

By Oak and Thorn
A Record of English Days

ISBN/EAN: 9783337279592

Printed in Europe, USA, Canada, Australia, Japan

Cover: Foto ©Andreas Hilbeck / pixelio.de

More available books at **www.hansebooks.com**

BY OAK AND THORN

A Record of English Days

BY

ALICE BROWN

BOSTON AND NEW YORK
HOUGHTON, MIFFLIN AND COMPANY
The Riverside Press, Cambridge
1896

TO

MY GOOD COMRADES

WHO

SHARED THE FOOTPATH WAY

CONTENTS

" Then follow you, wherever hie
The traveling mountains of the sky,
Or let the streams in civil mode
Direct your choice upon a road;

" For one and all, or high or low,
Will lead you where you wish to go:
And one and all go night and day
Over the hills and far away!"

ROBERT LOUIS STEVENSON.

BY OAK AND THORN

IN PRAISE OF GYPSYING

AND now, with the youth of the year, hath come a strange longing upon the hearts and within the veins of all creatures living, and one born to a climate of unchanging peace would scarcely know what it might portend. For there works a sweet languor and at the same time a quickening within the blood; the spirit is given over to melancholy, and alternately to joyance, and the lips fit themselves easily to snatches of old song. Conscience is dead within us, or, if it speak, it is to fret us, though listlessly, that we stay indoors while the apple is forming within the green of the bud, and while columbines nod bravely, and over-sea the may is whitening well her fairy smock, spread lavishly upon green hedges. "What avails it," we cry, "that we labored all winter within the

prisoning of four dull walls? Our books
are written, our canvas lies wet, our
songs are sung; yet what living soul is
the better for our travail? Children are
we that play at shaping a creation of our
own, while without us the ever-mutable
yet ever-living makes unto itself red
sunsets, and with one spring-attired birch-
tree set against a background of pine
puts to shame all the conceptions of
art." And therefore, sick with the vanity of our seriousness, do we turn the
hearing inward and listen to the throbbing of swift-pulsing currents; and their
measure is that of a jocund march drawing us ever onward. Where, we know
not, and if we have but one drop of
blessed gypsy blood, that, like moving
quicksilver, doth inform the whole, we
care not; for, as one great among wizards
truly declares, "to travel hopefully is a
better thing than to arrive." (They that
know not spring may finish the line, to
the effect that "the true success is to
labor," but we who be gypsies will toss
this tiresome tag into the next thicket.
It smacks of the school-room, and all
moralizing have we forsworn.) And
ever at this season, when one has tuned

his ear to listen, the voice of bird and tree is, "Come!" and the sailing clouds cry, "Follow!" Memories don brave attire, masquerading as hopes, and step gayly forward to the tune of "Summer is icumen in." Let Emerson assure us that he who stays at home hath as great a share of the universe as he that travels abroad, and let Whittier equalize the wanderer's lot with that of him

"who from his doorway sees
The miracle of flowers and trees," —

their words are empty air; we give courteous acquiescence, yet from the moment when the tassel droops first on the alder to that when the last crimsoned maple leaf flutters down the wind, Nature herself — contained within the fragile vial of man's being — contradicts it. "Come!" she cries to us, as to the young birds on the rim of the nest, "Come — and follow!" What loving sympathy have we now for that happy band who, in one guise or another, but never that of conformity to the world - discerning eye, "house by the hedge," and make their rallying note,

"To the wood then, to the wild: free life, full liberty!"

3

Among us who can seize upon such heritage of delight, books shall be forsworn ; but if, in some moment of weakness, we long for the old vice of print, let it be that excellent work, the life of Bampfylde-Moore Carew, commonly called the King of the Beggars. Born respectably, the son of a rector (alas ! good youth, he would fain have had it otherwise), he followed his star to the greenwood, and there out-gypsied the gypsies. A love and longing not to be withstood marched ever before him, and like joyous pioneers cleft the way to his desires. He joined the gypsies ; he received the crown of virtuous ambition, and became their king. Lustily rang the inauguration ode at his crowning, whereof one line containeth the whole philosophy of summer :

"This is Maunders' holiday !"

Maunders (beggars), their holiday is eternal while the sun shines and the grass grows, and we, if we be worthy, may pick up the crumbs of their festival. Glorious and historic precedent have we for our vagrom desires. When Æneas became aweary of philandering, or was suddenly alive to the divine message

(and who can tell, in the case of any
mortal man, whether he be moved by
gods or *ennui?*), when this same paste-
board hero was minded to leave the
pedestal whereon poor Dido had set him,
what did he do? Marry, he kicked down
the altar, smoking with the sacrifice of
her queenly devotion, scattered the ashes
of her hopes, and *set sail!* Potent
phrase! The mariners pulled with lusty
will, the sea sparkled, a jolly breeze
sprang after, and Æneas was safe on
waves no salter than Dido's tears, yet
under a sun more beguiling than her
smiles. Stay - at - homes were ever de-
puted to do the weeping; be warned,
dear pilgrim, and buckle on your shoon!
Ulysses of wily memory — was he animated solely by a virtuous desire for
home-made cakes and ale, in quitting
Circe and Calypso, and their bribes of
gilded ease? Rather had he tired of
island life; he was ready to be up and
away. Theseus, deserter of Ariadne
and the Isle of Naxos! it was never in
obedience to the gods, say I, that he
showed so clean a pair of heels. Mi-
nerva appeared to him, reads the tale.
Possibly, yet only after he had been

moved by dreams of a swifter flight, a more adventurous way than that of him who has newly enslaved himself to love. " Bind me with no fetters, not even in the prisoning of rosy arms !" sang his Viking soul. Jason was a shrewd merchant, a hardy adventurer, yet sought he chiefly the Golden Fleece, or to cool the fever of his youth ?

Strange suspicions awaken in us when the distance wooes, and spring airs blow soft ; doubts, all unwonted, of the true values of ancient tales. At such moments even the Crusader seems not so much enkindled with the passion for rescuing earth's holy spot, as a wanderer moved by vague desire of foreign lands and sweetly new experience ; one who, though spendthrift of time and strength, would yet store up, for his gray and broken age, a casket of golden memories. He was the bird of passage of a prayerful time ; his scallop shell, his staff and sandals, were symbols not only of a yearning faith and abiding constancy, but of a natural delight such as those hemmed in by "four gray walls" can never know. To run the finger further down the margin of the past is to find —

what burning names, what wild adventure! Elizabeth queened it in England when she would fain have taken sword in hand, and sailed the sea with the best of her merry men, killing the Spaniard, and drinking deep of the desire of life. They fought for crown and faith (and booty, — let not that be forgot!); but though the peace of Christendom was the laurel leaf for which they held life but as "a pin's fee," not the less did they pursue continual change for pure love and for the quieting of their perturbèd spirits. This was the *Wanderjahr* of their time, counterpart of the Age of Chivalry; they who would truly live, lived on the wing, and Fortune was with them, and their own stout hearts their best companioning.

And for us? There are no sacred tombs to deliver, no Hesperides in imagined view, and perhaps not even one soul to be rescued and deserted in the light-hearted fashion of our mythic forbears; but not for that will we fold our hands at home, and live the life of niderings and them that be easily content. This moment of the opening bud is that for which we have endured our months

7

of servitude. The chrysalis hath ful-
filled its destined use, and now the creature hath his wings to fly away, and soar
or flutter as his nature bids. We will go
forth, not perchance like a wiser race,
to hang odes on the blossoming cherry,
but to seek that beauty which the hand
of man hath not made, and the secret
of which no cunning can divine. To lie
beneath the open sky, to mark the
rhythm of murmuring treetops, and face
the wild rose unshamed, in that our lives
have grown serene and natural as hers,
— that shall be our desire and our delight. If we may sail the seas that have
cradled heroes, and walk the shores of
golden memories, we are blest indeed;
but whatever be our station, let us go
out, whether to sit among the limes and
yews of Stratford churchyard, or in a
New England pasture, tippling on fragrance and lulled by the foolish bees.
Somewhere, somehow, we will wander,
look and listen, and ringing in our ears
shall be one or another majestic chant,
like the solemn prophecy of a greater
hope and a more splendid journey : —

"My purpose holds
To sail beyond the sunset, and the baths

Of all the western stars, until I die.
It may be that the gulfs will wash us down:
It may be we shall touch the Happy Isles,
And see the great Achilles, whom we knew."

FEW are the pens of perfect technique, and only such may fitly couple the ethereal with the grossly utilitarian. So by a good-fortune not always regnant, even in the happy world of verse, it fell to Aldrich to link the praise of "dreamy words" and "very pleasant eating." His was the good word, for he was born to see and sing; but ours shall be the joyous deed, especially when we have set forth on pilgrimage to inherit the earth. On such days, far from the mahogany-tree we left behind us, every homely act gains a new significance; and unfamiliar food fits itself, not only to the nourishment of corporeal particles, but to that spiritual life wherewith we draw our only vital breath. So that it becomes the wise to refrain from considering eating as an exact science, — so much nitrogen, so many units of energy, — and to merge it into a contemplative and poetic delight, unknown to him who only eats to live. On such a topic it is impossible to speak impersonally, or to shield one's self behind the egotistical bulwark of the editorial *we*. It is necessary to betake us individually to the small go-cart of the first person; for who ever ate altruistically, or chewed the cud of a foreign flavor, save to his own self-limited delight? To speak straitly, then, as a unit whose yea would fain, in this matter, be simply yea, I frankly avow that my shallop of joy in English travel was upborne upon an ever-buoyant wave of table-delight. The earliest May-blossom, the first English daisy, quivered in white before my seeking eyes, wraith-pictures from the land of dreams; the first English gooseberry tart stood forth a more substantial but no less joyous herald of welcome to a soil whose heroes have ever held tankard and trencher in honorable repute. What fruit this side the land of pure delight can rival the English strawberry? the only sort of immortal joy you can buy by the pound. And though, alas! no purveyor shall henceforth bring us tribute from the garden of "my lord of Ely," so also nothing short of an irresponsive palate can deprive us of that flavor underlying the rosy

flesh even in the days of Tyrant Richard. I ate my first strawberry from a
little basket (you know the shape, dear
pilgrim!) in a field bordering the Nun's
Walk, on the banks of Itchen. And so
corpulent was the fruit, so grown beyond
all reason, though lacking nothing of
tenderness and fragrance, that we measured its bulk with a wisp of grass, and
sent the boastful girth home to one who
would have been with us, had the gods
dealt tenderly. In Devon, more straw-
berries, some eaten in an exquisite dairy-
shop off the cathedral close, at Exeter,
their nectarous juices enriched and softened with clotted cream, and set off by
cloying junket, as a country lass by her
hot-house sister. It was at Ilfracombe,
later in this progress of delight, that a
matron, pink of cheek and gown, gave
us the recipe for the clotted cream, most
delectable product of the red-soiled south.
But you cannot "bring home the river
and sky." You shall have Devon cattle,
and learn the tricks of the dairy from a
thousand years' inheritance, else your
cream will turn out a plain and wholesome compound of the taste of scalded
milk: and no charm, even the specific

furnished the guileless Annie by Coun-
sellor Doone, shall avail you.

It was in a little Warwick shop that I
was first made one with weal and 'am
pie, that concoction so cunningly tra-
duced by Sam Weller that no one may
eat it, from his time forth, without a
premonitory shudder.

"'Weal pie,'" said Mr. Weller, solilo-
quizing, as he arranged the eatables on
the grass. "'Wery good thing is a weal
pie, when you know the lady as made it,
and is quite sure it ain't kittens.'"

But the verdict of the American palate
was altogether favorable. "Much like
the British character," says retrospect.
"Solid and satisfying, and 'pleasant, too,
to think on!'"

At Dulverton, immortal halting-place
of John Ridd as he rode home from
school across the moors, on the occasion
of his standing up like a pixy in the dark,
and shouting prophetic defiance to the
returning Doones, a culinary disappointment lay coldly in wait. We would fain
have duplicated John Fry's order, —
"'Hot mootton pasty, zame as I hardered
last Tuesday;'" but there was no time
for the cooking, and we went away with

the sacred rite undone. Moreover, not in
all Devon did mention of pickled loaches,
the love whereof first led little John into
the Doone Valley, do more than rouse a
wondering look on the face of the myth-
ignoring inhabitants. But, we might
have asked, to what end should Devon
kitchens exist, save for the perpetuating
of sacred lore and setting before the reverent palate hot collops of venison, such
as were approved by its tutelary giant,
and all else that went to the nourishing
of his mightiness? Shame on him who
would remove one guidepost of the culinary past, one viand embalmed in story!
Let his name be anathema, though he
invent a thousand modern trifles, or a
sauce to outrival Worcestershire. For
no tickling of the palate under new com-
binations can compensate for the starving
of the soul.

You who have trodden English by-
paths and fallen in with ancient ways,
did you ever eat English buns without
a jingling mental accompaniment to the
tune of the old nursery rhyme? And
though you consumed them luxuriously
in the London A B C shops, or made
your touring staff that other variety to

be found, yellow with saffron, beside the
Cornish sea, were they not soul-satisfying and plummy ? I charge you, O seekers of inward joy, by all the past eating
you have ever done, to your own enlarge-
ment of vision, that, when you come
upon a classic dish, you pass it not by.
And north and south the traditionary
riches of the kitchen shall be yours. For
in Derbyshire, you shall eat Bakewell
pudding, of the genus tart, having, as
one greater than the world of realists
hath said, "a sort of mixed flavor of
cherry-tart, custard, pineapple, roast tur-
key, toffy, and hot buttered toast." At
Banbury, or possibly farther afield among
the Shakespeare haunts, you may purchase the unholy Banbury cake, which is
no less than a superlatively rich mince
turnover, evidently without the meat,
but compensating for all conventional
lack by fruits and spices. Without
doubt it will trouble your dreams, for
no Banbury cake ever did its spiriting
gently; but in the end, when absence
shall have softened every harsh detail
of that English journey, it will linger, a
spicy savor, in your happy memory. You
shall eat haggis and scones in Scotland,

roast goose and apple-sauce wherever
you can get them, star-gazing pie in
Cornwall (filled with pilchards, their innocent heads protruding above the crust),
and go, like all your generation and the
fathers of the English-speaking race, to
Richmond, to dine at the Star and Garter,
upon whitebait and Richmond maids-of-
honor. You shall eat chad from Lake
Windermere, in memory of the Roman
legions who carried that royal family
thither; and everywhere shall you bow
down before old England's roast beef,
though she import it from Australia or
America, and so hold historic lien upon
it by courtesy only. Her chops, of a
thickness and succulence unknown in
the golden West, shall tell their own
story of growth in fields fat with yellow
mustard blooms, where the innocent
sheep hourly nibble and munch, unconscious that such sunny joy is decreed
but for the flavoring of tissue. All this
may you have for the paltry exchange of
shillings; but, as for the salmi put together by the weaving fingers of Becky
Sharp for her bamboozled brother-in-law,
even the prince of the power of imagination shall fail to resuscitate that. Such

salmis are dead and gone with Becky
and the snows of yester-year.

No bread and beer in England mingle
such savor of lovely past and present as
the bit and sup making up the dole of
Saint Cross Hospital, and served to any
wayfarer at the open hatch. There, in
tantalizing nearness to the custodian's
blue china within the lodge (china which
is not for you!) and neighbored by the
green quadrangle where the gowned
brethren go pottering about in serene
relinquishment of care, you linger at
will (so you come but once a day!) sip-
ping your horn cup as it were elixir.
This is no bread and beer alone, but a
heartening food, a magic draught, holding
all the flavor of that idyllic walk, when,
awed with peace and "soft as bees by
Catherine Hill," you cross the meadow
from Winchester by ways parcel - gilt
with golden mimulus, where the river
dreams of gentle things and the breath
of cattle scents the air. For me, too,
it keeps the memory of that day when
I first bent over the opulent, homely
flower-beds, and asked the brother whose
art was gardening what name he gave
the ladies'-delights cosily settled there.

"Lublidles," he returned, in some courteous interest that one could call them otherwise.

Shakespeare's love - in - idleness! In some spots — be thankful ! — the world does not move.

What memories are ours of the first crab essayed at Seaton, where we attacked him gingerly, not knowing his kind, and mentally repelling the simile of ossified spiders ! The waiter stood by, meantime, fraternal over a maiden effort and solicitous for the fame of Devon. His self-forgetful joy when the venture was made and we vowed our fealty then and there to the worthy crustacean — that was something to see! What shall despoil us of the day when we halted before a mediæval-seeming shop near old Bristol's Christmas Steps, and read the longing on the faces of three children standing there without, staring hard at the winkles, cockles and mussels in the window ?

"Which are the nicest ?" asked we with the humility of the non-elect.

"Mussels, miss !" rang the concerted shout, whereupon tuppence each turned the loiterers into mussel-eating monarchs.

THE FOOD OF FANCY

Two of us will never set eyes on the
London barrows loaded with like marine
delicacies without choking reminiscence
of a certain expedition planned, gloated
over in the night-watches and never accomplished. For we had invited a lady
of social high degree, who knows only
poetic and fashionable London, and for
whom the City is a myth, to vouchsafe
us one day wherein to show her the
World and the joys thereof. She should
ride on the tops of 'buses, she should be
presented to the Duke of Suffolk's head,
resident in the Minories, salute Gog and
Magog, and pause before the tree "at the
corner of Wood Street." But alas! in
a moment of ill-judged prophecy we referred to the mussels of Shoreditch to
be purchased from a barrow and dipped
in the public vinegar ; and being daintily
nurtured, thenceforth she would none of
our unholy pranks.

Milk is no uncommon beverage, yet
sometimes it has a taste of all Arcadia.
One June day when we were on the
march brought us to the Welsh paradise
of Montgomery, where Magdalen Her-
bert's castle heights are standing, crown-
less, wonderful. We were entering the

village foot-sore but never weary (and with no time for food, for there were many miles to tramp, that night, before we got home to our den, O) and there, providentially meeting us, came a clean woman driving a clean cow into a tidy yard. Never was bargain more swiftly sealed. She disappeared to bring two bright glasses and a quart measure. She milked and we, throned on a strip of turf, drank, while round about us thronged the village children, solemnly classifying two gaitered, short-skirted and apparently hollow monsters. That was milk such as they drink on Olympus when Hebe serves, though possibly only a cut above the draughts permanently on tap, for a penny or for love, at farm-house doors.

We are wise, we who go gypsying. We have known what it is to find mushrooms on the Stratford Road and to smell them, one strange Dorset day, through a choking mist through which the trees seemed walking toward us as we went. How good must elf-men be, we said, to set a banquet there for such as are born with eyes and nose! We have learned the soul-satisfying quality of raw turnips, for we fed thereon, one hungry, happy afternoon in Kent. We have lived.

Certain harmless fictions dominate the English mind regarding the national "victuals." Smile over them, and enjoy the more. You may long for apples, and "seek all day ere you find them;" for the English apple, as it appears in the market, is prone to show a degree of hardness known to us in no article of food save sugar gooseberries. "I like a good tasty apple meself," said an English wench, setting white teeth into a knurly pippin; "something to bite on!" She had it; a baby foreordained to gums might have cut molars upon it. You may ask plaintively for vegetables, in ordering your dinner, to be answered daily, with a naïve air of delighted discovery, "Potatoes!" And should you hint at a larger ambition, a nobler quest, you may count yourself proud and happy if the omnipresent pea is an available candidate, albeit the only one. There may be set before you a loathsome and greasy compound with the encouraging dictum, "This is an American doughnut!" (An historic introduction: "Pudding — Alice; Alice — pudding. Remove the pudding!") But though, for honor's sake, you deny the fallacy, you shall eschew its ocular proof. Everywhere seek out the native and historic dish; and some happy day, if Fortune fawn upon you, roasted crabs may hiss for you in the bowl, and you shall have saffron in the warden pies.

WE would hear the nightingale, but, more slenderly equipped than John Burroughs in the same fine quest, we had not the certainty of making literary capital out of our ill-success. For us failure was failure : a handful of the summer's gold irretrievably wasted. At Warwick, sure of place "and time agreeing," we made careful inquiry where the bird of wonder might be sought. According to the popular voice, the woods were full of nightingales ; I remember writing home, in a fit of emulous extravagance, that the tongues thereof daily served the castle lord and lordlings for breakfast. "Go down on the bridge, miss, at nine o'clock," said the optimistic landlady. "They do sing there most beautiful. 'Know one when you hear him?' Yes, indeed, miss! You can't mistake a nightingale!" Like all who love their gloriously mediæval and frankly dirty Warwick as she may be loved, we were accustomed to make a worshipful pilgrimage down past the

castle at twilight, chiefly to steal dreams
from one pink rose hanging high on the
castle wall ; and so it came about that
our observance appropriately ended with
the bridge and the greater quest. That
rose held strange emphasis in those Warwick days ; it played a part as real and
wonderful as the rôle of princess in tales
of fairydom. Little rosy breaths came
from her petals, grew into clouds of fan-
tasy and enveloped us. Our minds walked
dimly in a morning haze. We imagined
much about her, as one may about a rose.
She suggested to us her who seemed to
us then the Fairest of Women, and we
made our lady Countess of Warwick
(Cophetua's immortal maid !) hung there
in her sweet deserving upon the antiquity
of the house like that rose upon the stabile
wall. And though I have been there
since and the dirty white peacock flaunts
himself with the same ill-judged vanity,
and not one bourgeoning spray is less on
the ruined bridge without the gates,
Warwick Castle is never the same to me ;
for that one rose is gone, and no sister
flower could ever take her place. So we
dreamed until the dusk enfolded us, and
then went happily on to the bridge, stout-

hearted in desire and belief. There we paced and leaned and lingered, dallying with dampness and grave in discussion. The question was of mighty import, and always the same. When that liquid note was once entrapped, should we too find it and remember it *jug, jug?* We were wise, that summer. We knew how vital it was, how much more to be desired than great statecraft, to know whether her lamenting did so run, or whether it must melt into some strange wild note too untamable for even poets' paraphrasing. We need not have striven. The long summer twilights passed : the skies paled, and faded into dusk. Defeated seekers of a wealth more to be desired than El Dorado, there was nothing for us but to creep home, chilled and vanquished, to bed. Then it was that we bethought us of confiding in an all-knowing cab-driver, and his hopefulness put discouragement to shame. " Nightingales, miss?" quoth he. "Yes, miss, I know exactly where they sing. A mile or so out of Warwick is a lonely bit of road, and they hold regular concerts there. I went by last night, and they were a-singing away like everything. I could

take you out, miss, for 'arf a crown!"
Was ever tempting bait more cunningly
offered? We were caught, and that
night at ten o'clock, John, with a friend
on the box (both faithfully dressed to
represent Rogue Riderhood villains),
drove up in state. I have not yet been
able to decide why these two beguilers
of the American purse came thus dis-
guised. They had pulled their hats low
over their eyes, they had tied flaring
handkerchiefs about their necks, and had
turned up their collars at a murderous
angle. They may have had some exalted
idea of a practical joke; they may have
been afraid of the damp. We rattled
away, and John asked us respectfully, yet
with meaning, if there were not frequent
murders in America; he told us folk-
tales of horror, and then, at the moment
when my spinal marrow was properly
chilled, drew up the horse, on a lonely
bit of road, and announced, sepulchrally,
"This is the very place!" I had nearly
shrieked, "O, save me, Hubert, save
me!" but I remembered the nightingale,
and held my peace. Whether the nightingale was also mindful of us I know not,
but he was silent, too. For one hour we

sat there, and then drove slowly homeward, cold and depressed, our base guides
assuring each other, by the way, that
never, in all their lives, had they heard
of such a circumstance; still did they
insist that nightingales were always making musical clamor at that particular
spot.

With saddened hearts, we relinquished
the quest; but one night, at Stratford,
sitting in the coffee-room of the Red
Horse Inn, we mentioned our forlorn
pursuit before two young English boys.
They were knightly souls and ready.
They knew well where Philomel lamented
on the Warwick Road, and there would
they lead us, if we chose to go. Instantly
we were afoot with them in the moonlit
dusk, where the hedgerows smelled of
bloom, talking until the way grew lonely
(and so provocative of hope), and learning
something, I am persuaded, even in that
short space, of the finely tempered fibre
in little English lads. I cannot remember what they said; only that they were
very frank and very courteous (grown-up
and bookish, too, as compared with our
American children, using fine-spun words
and phrasing with an absolute lack of pre-

tense) and that they breathed the essence of all that is rarest in their nationality. Had it been this year of grace, 1896, I should here assert that they had neighbored and played with the boys and girls of "The Golden Age." One passport to their consideration seemed to be the fact that, as Americans, we were indubitably the countrywomen of Mr. William Winter. They had rowed with him on the Avon; he had evidently passed the silent and terrible scrutiny of a boy's ideals and been approved.

On and on we walked, fields on either side, and sweetness of summer all about. We talked less and less; we listened, expectant. A lonely corn-crake cried in the distance, — sound inharmonious, yet fitted to the darkness and the hour. And then — listen!

"How thick the bursts come crowding through
    the leaves!
        Again — thou hearest?
        Eternal passion!
        Eternal pain!"

No region short of Arcadia was ever
blest with historian more enthusiastic
than Charles Kingsley whenever he
touched upon Devonshire, her charms or
her story; then was his pen dipped in
illuminating colors, and he traced the
outline of her beauties on a page that
must endure until the memory of Devon
lads no longer thrills the romance-loving
heart. When guide-books wax eloquent
over this fair county, and dry historic
mention broadens into a sweep of verbal
imagery, then are the paragraphs hedged
between telltale quotation marks, and
a footnote points to Kingsley as the
source of such just laudation. His sympathy was perfect; the light of his genius
seems to brighten every golden thread in
the fabric of her story; and the traveler
who loves such an unfailing lover can
scarcely do better than to visit these
happy haunts with "Westward Ho!"
and the "Prose Idylls" in hand, as poetic guidebooks. Unlike many a memo-

rable spot, this has a beauty that is all its own, holding a peculiar power over the human spirit. Not only do the pages of its history rouse the heart to quicker pulsations by their review of the days when there were giants, but even the face of nature seems here significant. Devonshire may be "relaxing," as the neighbors of Bow Bells declare, with fine and almost depreciatory inflection, but nevertheless every breath within its borders inevitably exhilarates all who love a hero. The English Midlands spread out into a fair garden, beautified by the hand of man, and gaining grace from his necessities. Devonshire is all warm luxuriance, rolling waste, and stormy breaker. Its moorland wastes spread on and on, clothed only by coarse grass, heath, and furze; but its clefts and chasms are enriched by a marvelous fern growth, and cooled by clear mountain streams holding a multitude of fish within their limpid shallows. Dartmoor, like Salisbury Plain, is one of nature's high altars, to be approached with reverence and dread. A broad expanse, waste and wonderful, it lies like a sea caught in commotion and fixed in everlasting repose. The touch of cultivation has never disturbed its bosom, yet is it a storehouse of varied wealth. The antiquary may ponder long, unsatisfied, over its gigantic mounds and rocky remains, the fisherman fill his creel from its waters, and countless sheep nibble the unfenced pasturage ; but he whom it most delights is the pilgrim who fares along its ways, mindless of aught save shifting cloud beauties and the outline of the billowing hills. What treasure-house of form and color can match the English sky? Taken at its sunniest, here arches no crystal vault of blue, but one diversified by an ever-changeful pageant made from sunlit feather-down and clouds the color of a dove's gray wing, — glorified, nevertheless, by sapphire intervales. Such a procession of airy loveliness awakens a wondrous sympathy in Dartmoor below. Over its tors sweep the shadows, chased by a light that turns the heather to rose, and transforms the coarse grass to a fabric of warm yellow. One hollow lies scowling in darkness ; and lo ! beside it a hill smiles, and then laughs outright under a golden shaft of sun.

My own course over the moor led from

the little village of Chagford to Tavi-
stock, thence to seek Plymouth; and
when I set foot in that historic town, I
felt the tightening of Kingsley's grasp
upon my hand. "Come," he seemed
to say; "here was set the tiny stage
whereon great parts were played, as if
only Olympus were to be auditor and
judge. Come, and keep reverent silence;
read and remember!"

Plymouth is a town born for the perpetual flaunting of England's glory. It
sits in well-defended pride, looking calm-
ly over the waves which are Britannia's
own, and saying in every line of wall
and fortress, "Behold my impregnable
strength!" Should you, on arriving
there, confide to some inhabitant your
desire for a pleasant walk, he will say
substantially although not perhaps in the
eccentric diction of one kindly woman,
"Oh, the 'O, my lady, — you must go to
the 'O!" Half a mile from the station
brings one to this Hoe, or highest part
of the esplanade and pleasure-grounds
bordering the water, and themselves
locked in a wonder of stone outwork and
coping. Straight across the sound to the
south runs the breakwater, binding the

waves in such beneficent yet stony fetters that they lie tranquil and hospitable before the incoming mariner. Fourteen miles out stands the Eddystone Lighthouse, on the site of an earlier triumph of engineering, at whose firmness even its great projector, Smeaton, may have wondered, as morning after morning he climbed the Hoe, to exult as he found the tower still piercing the sunrise mist. The tale of the Eddystone Light has been one of varied tragedy. The first lighthouse erected there was washed away, and the second burned. Smeaton's stood the shock of wind and water for over a century, and then, having been removed on account of its insecure base, and replaced by the present structure, was set up on the green-carpeted Hoe, a perpetually honored pensioner. Companioned by it, and overlooking fortress and wave, stands, counterfeited in bronze, the hero of the deep, the scourge of Spain, Sir Francis Drake, about whose memory clings to-day a legendary glory, which, recited by old Devon dames at the hour when the thoughts of kid and old woman turn homeward, brings a parlous creeping along the spine even in

such as are able to summon also that
expression known in the older novels as
"a skeptical smile." Who can wonder,
after reading Drake's exploits, that Spain
held him to be no man, but devil? He
had a soul perpetually drunken with belief in self and a passionate love of action;
he was one of those who do, not the
things they can, but what they will; and
more than all, like Napoleon in his happier days, he had a star. His actual
doings read like fairy tales; but better
than them all do I love the folk-lore indicating his place in the common mind,
that afterglow sure to depict a vanished
sunset more faithfully than painter's
brush or poet's pen. Was she not a
prudent dame, the Spanish favorite who
refused to join a water-party with Philip
of Spain, even at the risk of offending
her sovereign, because she feared "El
Draque," that water dragon who, by force
of his magic arts, might be anywhere
at a moment's notice, — now in Europe,
now in Prester John's dominions? It
was he who brought water down into
Plymouth from clear mountain sources,
by the simple process of obtaining a
grant from the queen, and the good-will

of certain influential persons through whose ground it must run. But did such commonplace means suffice for the popular imagination? Not in the least. Sir Francis mounted his great black horse, and rode up into Dartmoor. There he found a spring by Sheep's Tor. He beckoned, it followed, and, as he galloped down into Plymouth town, the stream, a docile Jill, came tumbling after.

"And fine would have been the Diversion," says a worthy chronicler, "when the Water was brought somewhere near the Town, to have seen how the Mayor and his Brethren, in their Formalities, went out to meet it, and bid it welcome hither; and that being thus met, they all returned together, the Gentlemen of the Corporation accompanied with Sir Francis Drake, walked before, and the Stream followed after into the Town, where it has continued to do ever since."

Though some give Sir Francis the mere credit of taking the contract for the waterworks, which had been previously planned by others, he is never forgotten in his capacity of Plymouth's cup-bearer. One loving custom of the town is its annual survey of the watercourse, amply described in a programme of the ceremony, dated July, 1891, — a bit of paper calculated, as it lies in the hand, to set one to dreaming of that heroic past with which it forms a solid link.

"At the Head Weir," says this quaint and delightful memorial, "the party being assembled, a Goblet filled with pure Water taken from the Weir by the Surveyor is handed by him to the Chairman of the Water Committee, who presents the same to the Mayor, and requests him to drink thereof, 'To the pious memory of Sir Francis Drake,' and passing the Cup from one to the other each drinks and repeats the same words. Another Goblet, being filled with Wine, is then presented by the Chamberlain to the Mayor, who drinks to the Toast — 'May the Descendants of him who brought us Water never want Wine.' Passing the Cup as before."

Then followed "Ye Fyshinge Feast," provided with trout taken from the stream, and concluded by toasts to the royal family, the mayor, and water committee, and topped by one imperishable custom. For "before separating," says the programme, "'Ye Lovynge Cuppe'

36

will be passed in pledge of 'Unity and Prosperity' to the Town of Plymouth." United may it stand, and prosperous as if Sir Francis yet reigned, its living dictator !

The story of Drake's marital influence is well suited to his reputed temperament and generalship. His second wife was Elizabeth Sydenham, of Combe Sydenham, Somerset; and before leaving her in the temporary widowhood entailed by one of his voyages, he threatened her with dire consequences should her fealty waver. Months stretched on in a weary chain, and the lady, believing him to be dead, reluctantly accepted another suitor. But just as they were setting forth to church, in the midst of a violent thunder-storm, a ball of iron a foot in diameter fell hot on the pavement and rolled between the astonished pair. As the impartial student of history will at once believe, the wronged husband had taken aim from the antipodes, and as usual hit his mark. "It is the token from Drake!" exclaimed the unwilling bride. "He is alive! I will not go to church." Nor did she, and Drake himself soon appeared to requite

her readiness in taking a hint. Some,
indeed, say that the incident occurred
while the two were merely plighted
lovers, but I tell the tale as 't was told
to me within the Devonshire borders.
Historians may be cheerfully allowed to
have it otherwise, but even their dictum
is less to be desired than the warm if
distorted memories of an auld wife's
brain.

One bit of gossip the worshipers of
Sir Francis would fain consign to the
lists of fiction, though it is set down by
sober John Prince in his "Worthies of
Devon." It seems that, like many a
lesser soul, the admiral was at one time
bitten by the fever of ancestry, and bor-
rowed, to speak in mildness, a coat of
arms belonging to Sir Bernard Drake,
head of an elder branch of the name,
from whose line his own descent could
not be traced. Sir Bernard naturally
resented the perching of this uninvited
guest on his family tree, and one day,
when the feud had waxed fiery hot,
within the verge of the court he gave
Sir Francis a box on the ear. Thereupon Elizabeth, jealous for her favorite
as only a woman can be, bestowed

upon Sir Francis a vainglorious coat of arms all his own, indicating symbolically his dominion over the world of waters, and at the same time cunningly flouting the elder line; for in the rigging of the ship adorning the crest was a wyvern, copied from the crest of Sir Bernard, but ignominiously hung by the heels. Nevertheless, one is inclined to think Sir Bernard had the best of the matter in his neat retort that " though her Majesty could give Sir Francis a nobler coat than his, she could not give him an antienter one."

Kingsley's vivid description of Plymouth as it was in 1588, when the Invincible Armada undertook the demolition of Protestant Christendom, is well rounded, in his portraiture of the men who were gathered in the town to await the arch enemy, by the picture of " a short, sturdy, plainly dressed man, who stands with legs a little apart, and hands behind his back, looking up with keen gray eyes into the face of each speaker. His cap is in his hands, so that you can see the bullet head of crisp, brown hair and the wrinkled forehead, as well as the high cheek bones, the short square face,

the broad temples, the thick lips, which
are yet firm as granite. A coarse, ple-
beian stamp of man, yet the whole figure
and attitude are that of boundless determination, self-possession, energy; and
when at last he speaks a few blunt words,
all eyes are turned respectfully upon
him, for his name is Francis Drake."

And there on Plymouth Hoe was he
playing at bowls when a sailor hurriedly
put in shore, to say that the enemy had
been sighted. The English, from lord
high admiral to common sailor, were
tired of waiting. They had grown uneasy over conflicting rumors and Elizabeth's weathercock advance and withdrawal, and even the leaders sorely
needed the solace of that match on the
green. Yet when the great word broke
upon the ear of Drake, what did he reply? That he would play out his game,
since there would afterwards be time
enough and to spare for beating the
Spaniard. But who would attempt re-
peating the after-story which many have
told so well? Suffice it for us to recall
the folk-version of the first scene in
the grand drama, wherein the winds of
heaven and the heroism of earth played

antiphonal parts. When the Spanish fleet appeared, say Plymouth dames, Sir Francis quietly called for a billet of wood and an axe. The stick he proceeded to chop into small pieces, which, as he threw them into the water, speedily became men-of-war; and these Devonian dragon's teeth (fraternal and beneficent, unlike the crop of old!) fell upon the enemy of Gloriana the Great, and straightway destroyed him.

At the right of the Hoe, a wilderness of greenery overlooking the sea, lies Mount Edgcumbe, wisely selected by the leader of the Armada for his own share of the spoils. He had an eye for beauty, this Medina Sidonia; and even at this late day, with all our sympathies enlisted on the winning side, we can but feel "the pity of it" that even so insolent an invader should thus have "loved a dream," though we smile, perforce, over old Fuller's ironical remark that "the bear was not yet killed, and Medina Sidonia might have catched a great cold, had he no other clothes to wear than the skin thereof." It is easy to picture the delight with which the sea-wearied eyes of the Spanish mariners must have rested on this royal spot. Sheer above the dimpling water rise mountainous cliffs, crowned by a noble growth of trees, and carpeted with sweet under-verdure. Mount Edgcumbe Park, where the public is permitted to wander on specified days, is a miracle of beauty. Tracts of woodland alternate with garden beds rich in color. Laurel and holly reflect the day in their shining leaves, and a wondrous giant hypericum stars the ground with bloom. The great estate is traversed by broad walks and winding paths, apparently due not to design, but to the errant will of some wanderer; and now and again, in skirting the cliff, you may look down into the summer sea, over the greenly wooded Drake's Island in the harbor. At happy intervals are lodge and cottage, where you may order delectable tea and plum-cake for sixpence, or ham and eggs (the bulwark of England's greatness) for another silver trifle. And if the sky, such of it as you can see through the treetops, smile upon you, and the typical sight-seer be not omnipresent, you will take the little boat again for Plymouth quay, after a dreamy half-day in the park, more alive than ever to England's beauty and Medina Sidonia's taste in real estate.

Were one to attempt a summary of Plymouth's notable days and names, he would find an American tourist's stay within its gates all too short for dwelling fitly upon associations of such magnitude. From that port set sail, in its golden days, an "infinite swarm of expeditions." Drake put forth from its harbor to circumnavigate the globe. Sir John Hawkins made it the initial point of his dark but masterful career. Sir Walter Raleigh's fleet set sail thence for the settlement of Virginia, and hither he returned, broken-hearted, from his last fatal expedition in quest of the golden city of Manoa. Sir Humphrey Gilbert went thence to Newfoundland, a voyage destined to stretch on into that other, infinite journey, illumined by the burning words, "We are as near heaven by sea as by land." From Plymouth, also, embarked, in 1620, those pilgrims who had left Holland for a bleaker but more desired haven. Quaint and dry are the early chronicles of the town, denoting a race of tough fibre, fit associates for the mariners whose names do so burn and flash upon the page. These were men who stood no more upon ceremony than old "Frankie Drake," and who could give and take such missiles of dry humor as might well be considered both danger- ous and deadly in their effect on friendly intercourse. Some of the stories con- nected with the early mayors recall the candor once prevailing in the pit of the English theatres. Shipley, being meek by nature and deportment, was popularly called "Sheepley," and evidently took no offense thereat. Farcy, who would have the world know that he was "gentleman born," struck the town clerk for not call- ing him "your Worship," and so was dubbed thereafter "Worshipful Farcy" by all the Plymouth *gamins*, perhaps even with the concurrence of their tough- hided fathers. Yogge, who was blamed for belittling his office by bearing his meat home from market, returned with sturdy good wit, "It's a poor horse that won't carry its own provender!" But of all the legends connected with these robust city fathers, none better shows us the stuff of which they were made than a true tale of Mayor Dirnford, who, in 1455, in church "on his opening day,"

had a fit of apoplexy. No such slight incident, however, could really disturb his
Worship. He came out of it with dignity,
as from a recognized part of the services,
and at dinner ate Michaelmas goose, saying grimly that the fit had given him an
appetite.

Of the beauty and strength of Plymouth at the present day, it would be
difficult to say too much. It includes
within its jurisdiction the sister towns
of Stonehouse and Devonport, all three
bearing the patent marks of military design and occupation. Look into the Cat-
water and Hamoaze, estuaries of the Plym
and Tamar, twin rivers of Plymouth, and
you shall find men-of-war and humble
merchant vessels. Go to Devonport, and
there you may seek the dockyards, en-
ticingly open to such foreigners as are
favored by the gods and the admiralty.
Though the days have long passed when
seafaring heroes trod the streets, Plymouth will disclose many a quaint corner
to such as are patient as well as curious :
witness, at least, the Barbican, where one
who fears not sea slime and good-natured
chaff may meet the fishing population at
dawn ; and also that eccentric auction

distinguished by the falling of every bid. What lover of the past could be misled by a garnished exterior? Yet if there be one thus "fond and foolish," let him in Plymouth seek out that square where so many stately buildings are congregated, and, ignoring their carven freshness, enter old Saint Andrew's Church. For there were the people at service, three hundred years ago, when a salute told the news that Sir Francis Drake had returned from the seas which "were a prison for so large a spirit," and drew forth men, women, and children to meet the victorious hero.

Another bit of earth where the loyal heart beats at thought of Kingsley and olden days is Clovelly, jewel dropped in a cleft of the rock, happy human nest builded close by the sea. The approach to this oddest corner of creation, past vestiges of a Roman encampment, gives no hint of the beauties on which the eye is presently to feed. The coach stops, apparently in a gentleman's park devoted to utilitarian ends ; and leaving care behind, in the shape of baggage, the traveler must thereupon take to his feet down a steep, rock-paved road, where all tourists fare alike, be they clad in frieze or gold. Suddenly, at a turn of the way, appears Clovelly Street, descending sharply in low, broad stairs laid with cobblestones. No carriage has ever profaned this stony staircase. Only the tiny hoofs of donkeys go clattering up and down; for it is Neddy who patiently toils under sacks of coal (trying, meanwhile, with gentle insistence, to " scrunch " the unwary traveler against the neighboring wall), or drags about sledges piled high with trunk and portmanteau, whose name here is legion. Flanking this declivitous way runs, on either side, a row of cottages, immaculate in whitewash, and adorned by fuchsia shrubs and geraniums. Halfway down stands the New Inn, its sign swinging across the street, — a little old-fashioned house, resplendent in old china, and kept in perpetual commotion by the influx of hungry excursionists, who come by boat and coach to flood the tiny village with admiring exclamations.

The quaintness of Clovelly is not all its charm; it wears, too, that of a wondrous beauty and delight. Lying as it does in an earth-cleft stretching down to the sea, it is fostered and overlooked by towering wooded cliffs, and, secure in humble contentment and sweetness of life, seems nowise inferior in merit to such natural pomp and magnificence. The little street wanders, in its progress to the water; once, perhaps twice, it boldly marches through the walls of a house (itself spanned by an archway above), and then after threading strange nooks and corners, where fishy smells mingle with the smoke which is Clovelly's natural breath, ends at the little harbor, — that harbor where, as Kingsley says, in the season of herring fishing so many boats set forth with song and prayer, some never to return. One scene, he tells us, would come upon him again and again: of "the old bay darkened with the gray coldness of the waterspouts stalking across the waves before the northern gales; and the tiny herring boats fleeing from their nets right for the breakers, hoping more mercy even from those iron walls of rock than from the pitiless howling wastes of spray behind them; and that merry beach beside the town covered with shrieking women and old men, casting themselves on the pebbles in fruitless agonies of prayer, as corpse after corpse swept up at the feet of wife and child, till in one case alone the dawn saw upwards of sixty widows and orphans weeping over those who had gone out the night before in the fullness of strength and courage."

Kingsley's father was rector of Clovelly during six of those years when the sensitive lad must have been very delicately responsive to new impressions. Under the mysterious spell of sea and cliff, he conned the pages of England's naval history, learning it through the heart rather than the mind ; for here did he catch the spirit of those men who made it glow and burn. From Devon air, her sunshine, waves, and rocks, rather than Hakluyt's Chronicles, was born his fiery sympathy with that heroic race who peopled the deep three hundred years ago. "Now," said he to his wife, on her first visit to Clovelly, "now that you have seen the dear old paradise, you know what was the inspiration of my life before I met you." His very spirit permeates the place; his name is there a household word.

"Did you know Mr. Kingsley?" I

asked a woman, beautiful with health,
and bearing the dignity of a sturdy
character, the wife of a "master mariner," to whom a humble stone was
erected in Clovelly churchyard. Evidently, that manner of speech was too
familiar as concerning a beneficent household deity. "We all saw him very often,"
she said with gravity. "As soon as he
came on his visits, he was in and out of
every house, as welcome as a bit of sunlight on a wet day, and asking how was
this one, and how was that, and had the
lads got home from sea? Ah, we loved
Mr. Kingsley!"

His happiest vacations were spent
here, sometimes as a guest at Clovelly
Court, and again in lodgings in a fuchsia-
decked house on Clovelly Street. Thence
he sailed to Lundy, or wherever a fisherman's lot might lead him, delighting his
keen eyes and reverent soul with God's
wonders dredged up from the deep. "I
cannot believe my eyes," was his home-
satisfied cry, on settling into a welcoming
nest. "The same place, the pavement,
the dear old smells, the dear old handsome faces again!"

The people who fill the picturesque

village houses are of a noble and dignified type. Clovelly women are tall and
shapely; the men bear in face and carriage unmistakable marks of thought and
feeling, and the children are marvels of
dark-eyed beauty. With such simplicity
and directness does the body here express
the soul that you may read daily, in
living lineaments, the story of a fine and
striving race. Life to these men is little
more or less than a year-long struggle
with the treacherous sea. So constantly
are they brought face to face with danger
that minor griefs are no longer present
to remembrance, and the desire of eternal life becomes to them all in all. Such
men were their dead-and-gone ancestors,
who fought the Armada, and went, "grim
or jocund," in quest of the "golden South
Americas;" such, in endurance and rigid
purpose, was Salvation Yeo, of "Westward Ho!" who was born in Clovelly
Street, in the year 1526, where his "father
exercised the mystery of a barber sur-
geon and a preacher of the people since
called Anabaptists." One noticeable circumstance, strange and pregnant, is that
Clovelly has no young men. They are
all at sea, serving their apprenticeship,

to come home for the innocent kisses of a dozen joyous women waiting on the quay, or to furnish new cause for the old ache, throbbing for the wanderer who may not return.

Clovelly may be approached through the Hobby Drive, a way of marvelous beauty skirting the top of the cliff, guarded by towering trees, and bordered with a lush undergrowth of ferns. From time to time in his course, the traveler will come upon a natural window in the leafy walls, — an airy space, whence he may overlook the blue sea, seek out Lundy's outline, severely simple, and in the distance the shadowy coast of Wales; and finally shall he receive the crowning vision of Clovelly herself, far below his eyrie, nestling in her flowery gorge, and drowsily indifferent to sea or wind. This road, a veritable fairy progress, belongs to Clovelly Court, where in the sixteenth century lived the Carys, one of whom figures so prominently among Kingsley's giants of action. They held it till the eighteenth century, when their branch of the family died out. And where now shall we seek a trace of the gallant Will who was one of that noble Brotherhood of the Rose, founded by Frank Leigh, worthy favorite of the Virgin Queen? Only Kingsley can rehearse his mimic history, though, if the trace of one of his forbears be cheering to the eye, the traveller may climb the height to the little church, to find a Cary's name in enduring brass. Another point of pilgrimage on the estate is Gallantry Bower, a steep cliff rising four hundred feet out of the sea, and commanding Hartland Point, Bideford Bay, and, stretching ever outward like a weird finger, Morte Point, where so many ships have gone down, — barren and dreadful Morte, which of all places on earth "God made last, and the devil will take first." Gallantry Bower, as Amyas says, is so named when one is on land, though you "always call it White Cliff when you see it from the seaboard." It has its appropriate legend ; for here, in a lonely tower, lived the fair lady of a Norman lord. She had a fine vantage point for surveying the world around, this victim of soft durance! Peace to her dust, — peace equal in measure to the skyful of beauty whereon she daily looked!

To go into lodgings at Clovelly is to

invite a possibility of becoming soon in-
terknit with the life of its kindly people.
In an angle of the stairlike street, almost
overhanging the quay, stands a bench
serving as council ground for the village
fathers. There, usually at twilight, when
the boats have come in and nets are dry-
ing, sits a row of grizzled mariners discussing the state — of the world, think
you? Nay, of the universe itself. One
bit of quaint philosophy, overheard during
such a twilight symposium, has lingered
in my ears, to sweeten many a tough
morsel of experience. "Well," said one
of these weatherworn sea-dogs, in the
tone of those who have drawn their own
conclusions from the inexplicable drama
called Life, "human nature's looking up
a bit; that's the only comfort." And
is human nature looking up even a bit,
Clovelly sailor, more familiar with the
deep than with human countenance, and
unpolluted by the grime of great cities?
It may be so; for out of the lips of men
unspotted from the world come often
truths more crystalline than those of science or statistics. In the village is sold
a photograph of Clovelly mariners, and
one face, a humorous, droll physiognomy,

at once strikes the attention. "And who is this?" I asked the sympathetic dealer. "Oh, that is poor old Captain Folly," said she, with a tear in her voice. "He died the other day. You must have been here." Yes, we were there in our lodgings at the head of the street, when Captain Folly was borne past by his brother mariners in their Sunday best; wearing also the becoming gravity of those who think gently and seriously of death, not during the one hour when it disturbs them at their avocations, but as children recognize the night as the inevitable foil of day. A solemn hymn was sung, strong voices sustaining the burden, and up the street to the little church was carried the old man whose journey was finished, and who slept, wrapped in honor and full of days, beneath the flag spread reverently upon his coffin.

Midway down the street stands — or stood — another old man, whose race is not soon to be run, judging from his apparent ability to keep feebleness and sorrow at bay. He is crippled, and waits at the domestic receipt of custom, ready to retail village gossip, and readier still to dispose, in a very self-respecting man-

ner, of the forthcoming shilling or sixpence. He is a trifle more cynical than
many of his brother mariners, this aged
man, the daily implication of whose life
is, "A penny, if you please," yet he
furnishes savor and spice in a godly
community.

But in order to find himself actually
near the heart of this simple folk, it is
the part of the reflective traveler to
attend chapel on Sunday, and not the
church. Such a service, once sought
out and followed, is never to be forgotten.
A rough hall in an obscure corner jutting
from the street, bare and uninteresting
as the old country schoolhouse, is filled
with worshipers, who at entrance and
departure make a mighty clattering on
the uncarpeted floor, and whose heart of
religious love raises their hymn-singing
to a resounding if strident chorus. What
lover of human expression would not
study reverently the faces in that lowly
chapel? Every eye fixed upon the
preacher, — a man who had somewhat
to say, a sermon full of hard and loving common-sense, — their earnestness
bespoke sheep worthy the guidance of
a faithful shepherd ; not such as feed

in grassy vales, but accustomed to stony
ways and mountain fastnesses, to storm
and night. One old man, whose every
look and gesture was of the sea, empha-
sized the prayers, from point to point,
with sonorous "amens." His soul drank
of the waters of life, said the recurrent
response ; this was his thanksgiving.

Eleven miles from Clovelly lies Lundy, from whose southeast edge rises the
Shutter Rock, terrible dramatic centre
of the tragedy so marvelously described
in "Westward Ho!" when, at the end
of Amyas Leigh's sixteen days' chase
of the Spaniard, the wind a destroying
angel, and lightnings and thunder the
messengers of an avenging heaven, Don
Guzman's ship was cast upon the rocks.
What traveler so painstaking as to seek
out Lundy will not remember at the
south that cliff overhanging the shore-
less cove and deep, dark sea, where blind
Amyas sat and drank in his vision of
the Spanish galleon, and her men "all
lying round her, asleep until the judgment day"?

"Don Guzman he never heeded, but
sat still and drank his wine. Then he
took a locket from his bosom ; and I

heard him speak, Will, and he said,
'Here's the picture of my fair and true
lady ; drink to her, Señors all.' Then he
spoke to me, Will, and called me right
up through the oar-weed and the sea :
'We have had a fair quarrel, Señor, and
it is time to be friends once more. My
wife and your brother have forgiven me,
so your honor takes no stain.' And I
answered, 'We are friends, Don Guzman ; God has judged our quarrel, and
not we.' Then he said, 'I have sinned,
and I am punished.' And I said, 'And,
Señor, so am I.' Then he held out his
hand to me, Cary, and I stooped to take
it, and I woke."

Lundy, in the days before steam had
rendered traveling "as easy as lying,"
was so inaccessible as to provoke the remark that the difficulty of getting there
was exceeded only by the difficulty of
getting away. Indeed, it is said that the
clergymen of five or six coast parishes
once made an excursion thither, and
were detained on the island over two
Sundays, to the exceeding dismay of
their waiting congregations, — an en-
forced season of retirement which, it is
hoped, the reverend gentlemen employed

for the good of their souls. The island is one of that brood of earth pigmies born to mightiness of garb and history. Its granite and slate defenses present an impregnable front to the Atlantic, and surging currents rage about it with a strength and fury to be surpassed only at Land's End. But once within its rocky gates, more smiling beauties greet the eye, for its vegetation is rich in that coloring which is the benison of sea air. Here heather and furze glow in rose and gold, the royal foxglove stands, and the sedum blesses the earth with bloom.

Lundy has had a checkered history, ever painted in gloomy and glaring hues. It can boast remains of a primeval population in flint and pottery, but few will care to trace its history further than the day of Sir Jordan de Moresco, its earliest recorded lord, who in the reign of Henry II. lived there a turbulent and piratical life, undaunted by king or peer, though his bit of land was declared forfeit to the crown. Of good old stuff were the Morescos, and they fought a valiant fight against law and order until 1242, when William of that name was seized and

hanged in London town. Thereafter,
Lundy became a favorite resort for
pirates, and was captured in turn by
French, Spanish, and even Turkish privateers. Seek its pages to-day, and you
will read the tamer sequel to so bold
a story: a few houses cluster at the
landing-cove, a lighthouse crowns the
plateau above; the scene is one of qui-
etude, broken only by the turmoil of
nature. On the upper plain lie also the
ruins of an ancient fortress known as
Moresco's Castle, forever tainted by the
blot of having sheltered a dastardly refu-
gee, Sir Lewis Stukely, Vice-Admiral of
Devonshire, and kinsman of Sir Walter
Raleigh, who through that craven means
came to the headsman's block. By this
Judas-like deed, Stukely earned the royal
favor, but irretrievably lost that of his
peers; and being vigorously insulted by
old Lord Howard of Effingham, he ran
whining to James and made complaint.
" What should I do with him?" queried
James. " Hang him? On my sawl, mon,
if I hung all that spoke ill of thee, all the
trees in the island were too few!" But
Stukely was to learn that treachery to a
friend and defection from a royal master

are two different offenses; for when, within a year, he was caught debasing the coin of the realm, there was nothing for it but flight before the winds of wrath. Into Devonshire hot-foot he hurried, and there was he resolutely boycotted; his own denied him, and the common people would give him "neither fire nor water." Again was he swept on by fate and furies to Lundy, and, seeking refuge in the old Moresco Castle, died there, "cursing God and man."

Not far from Clovelly lies Portledge, now the seat of the Pine-Coffins, and in Amyas Leigh's time the residence of that Will Coffin who made one among the lovers of Rose Salterne. The most prominent member of the old Coffin family figures boldly among Prince's "Worthies of Devon," and his life presents a pretty bit of incident scarcely to be told more vividly than in Prince's own diction, quaint and clear. This Sir William Coffin married, in the reign of Henry VIII., Lady Mannors of Derbyshire; "and residing, as is likely, with her on her Dowry in those Parts, he was chosen Knight of that Shire in the Parliment which began A. 21 K. Henry VIII.,

1529: In his way to which, there happened a remarkable Accident, not unworthy the relating, especially for the good Law it occasioned: Passing by a Church-yard, he saw a multitude of People standing Idle; he enquired into the cause thereof: Who reply'd, They had brought a Corse thither to be buried; but the Priest refused to do his office unless they first delivered him the Poor Man's Cow, the only quick goods he left, for a Mortuary. Sir William sent for the Priest, and required him to do his Office to the Dead: Who peremptorily refused it, unless he had his Mortuary first. Whereupon he caused the Priest to be put into the Poor Man's Grave, and Earth to be thrown in upon him; and he still persisting in his Refusal, there was still more earth thrown in, until the obstinate Priest was either altogether or well-nigh suffocated." This little drama led to an act of Parliament absolutely fixing the amount of mortuaries, and specifying the place of payment, so that no poor man was thereafter likely to be denied his last rites and resting-place. "All which," as Prince begs us to "make a note of," "Confirms the Observation,

That Evil Manners are often the Parent of Good Laws."

It were a pert and presumptuous pen which would attempt a description of Bideford after Kingsley has ticketed it with missal script, and laid it away for all time, in library records, as "the little white town . . . which slopes upwards from its broad tide-river paved with yellow sands, and many-arched old bridge where salmon wait for autumn floods, toward the pleasant upland on the west. Above the town the hills close in, cushioned with deep oak woods, through which juts here and there a crag of fern-fringed slate ; below they lower, and open more and more in softly-rounded knolls and fertile squares of red and green, till they sink into the wide expanse of hazy flats, rich salt-marshes, and rolling sand-hills, where Torridge joins her sister Taw, and both together flow quietly toward the broad surges of the bar, and the everlasting thunder of the long Atlantic swell." But the traveler who arrives there with the beginning of "Westward Ho!" warm in the memory will recall that, in the year 1575, Amyas Leigh, wandering home from

school along the quay, by the taverns
that lined the High Street, met there
two men telling strange tales of the gold
and gems of the New World, and the
marvelous adventures attendant on their
quest. These were Mr. John Oxenham,
of whose family Devonshire traditions
contain curious mention, and Salvation
Yeo. That the latter was a true Devonshire name "the bricks are alive to this
day to testify;" for in Bideford town I
saw it, not many months ago, on a pro-
saic and humble signboard. But though
syllables may defy the lapse of time, the
ancient taverns are gone, and the High
Street is a busy course of trade. Even
the old church, where Amyas and his
brother mariners gave thanks after their
wonderful voyage with Drake, has made
place for a new one. Only the muddy
Torridge flows daily in and out, alternat-
ing in yellow flats and dimpling water,
and Bideford bridge stands proud and
firm in the very outlines it wore when
the lad Amyas begged of Salvation Yeo
his carven horn. So old is this historic
bridge that no man knoweth the date
of its building. The most ancient existing seal of Bideford borough, dating

from the fourteenth century, bears its portrait; therefore must it have been alive and in good and honorable standing at that day. Its origin, like that of all truly self-respecting structures in Great Britain, is supernatural. It is recorded that the river was long ago crossed by a ford so dangerous that no stones could be laid there with any hope of permanence. Finally, however, the parish priest was told in a dream that a stone had been moved to a desirable spot in the stream, and there should the bridge be built. So this holy medium of communication 'twixt Heaven and Bideford, Sir Richard Gomard, or Gurney, revealed his vision to the bishop, who was pleased to "send forth indulgences and licenses" in order to enlist the good offices of his flock. They, obedient souls, gave abundantly, each according to his means. Many contributed money; the rich gave lands and the labor of their workmen, and the poor cheerfully offered the work of their hands, some for a week, and others, more prosperous or more zealous, for a month. That the succeeding bishops had the bridge's welfare in mind is indicated by the fact that

announcement was made not only from
the cathedral church of Exeter, but
throughout the diocese of Devonshire
and Cornwall, that those who would
promote and encourage this work "should
participate in all spiritual blessings forever." No wonder that the bridge became so rich as to hold its head high,
and bear itself with the dignity of a
landed proprietor, becoming, first and
last, "an inspired bridge, a soul-saving
bridge, an alms-giving bridge, an educa-
tional bridge, a sentient bridge, and last,
but not least, a dinner-giving bridge."

It was to the Grenviles that Bideford owed its early prosperity. The
first Grenvile of Bideford was a cousin
of the Conqueror; but the bright star of
that heroic family remains Sir Richard,
whose prowess is sung by every chanter
of Devon's fame, and who departed this
life in a swiftly-traced but ever-during
track of glory. For in the Revenge, off
Flores, with a hundred and twenty men,
he fought the Spanish fleet of fifty sail
and ten thousand men, from three in
the afternoon till daybreak next morning. But when, in that fury of battle,
more than a thousand of the enemy were

slain, while the Revenge lost but forty, when his boat was riddled through and through, and he himself was wounded, he would fain have blown up the vessel, and was forced to surrender only through want of ammunition. Three days after, he died of his wounds, saying in Spanish, that his captors might understand and know themselves defied to the last, "Here die I, Richard Grenvile, with a joyful and quiet mind, for that I have ended my life as a good soldier ought to do, who has fought for his country and his queen, for honor and religion."

Such was Richard Grenvile, who walks through "Westward Ho!" and the pages of less poetic history "a wise and gallant gentleman, lovely to all good men, awful to all bad men : in whose presence none dare say or do a mean or a ribald thing; whom brave men left, feeling themselves nerved to do their duty better, while cowards slipped away, as bats and owls before the sun." Well is he remembered as "the great Sir Richard, the pride of North Devon."

Kingsley's authority has been questioned for making Bideford one of England's chief ports in the sixteenth cen-

tury, though its halcyon days, beginning
under Elizabeth, rapidly brightened,
until its commerce with America and
Newfoundland became exceeding great.
French and Spanish privateers found
Bideford ships such rich booty that they
seized them in the very offing of the
Taw and Torridge, and ironically named
the spot " Golden Bay." But such flour-
ishing of commerce is a thing of the past,
for now the shipping trade of the Torridge is conducted mainly at the neighboring town of Appledore. Burrough
in Northam, where Kingsley fixed the
home of Amyas Leigh, has been for
centuries the seat of a family of the
name of Leigh, two of whom were seafaring men, and one, in Elizabeth's time,
" Chief Pilot of England." A member
of a luckless expedition to the Arctic
seas in the sixteenth century, he daringly
continued his voyage, even though a
companion ship was separated from him
by wind and weather. On he sailed
into the north, the region of perpetual
mystery, and, most undaunted of pioneers, entered the White Sea, naming
the North Cape by the way. Again, in
an insignificant vessel with a tiny crew,

he sailed triumphantly to a point within the Kara Sea, "beyond which," says Prince, "no navigator went until our own day." Truly Amyas the giant came of a goodly race, and one whose traditions bound him to heroic deeds.

Near the mouth of the Torridge lies a delightfully clean little town, a seaside resort of some pretension. This is Westward Ho, born of the great book to which the region is yearly indebted for crowding visitors. Though the town is modern, even amazingly so among such surroundings, its near neighbor is as old as — what? Let geology tell us. I had almost said, in the ignorant enthusiasm of the unscientific pilgrim, "as old as Adam." This neighbor is the Pebble Ridge, whose moaning told poor Mrs. Leigh, three miles away in Bideford town, that the sea and winds were rapidly rising, and that her boy, on his way to Ireland, would not sleep that night. The Ridge is simply a wide beach heaped with pebbles, the smallest larger than the fist, and on the day of my pilgrimage lying at rest beside a calm sea and under a smiling sky. But it is easily to be guessed that when the demons of air and

water strive together, these missiles of
the deep, wet with ocean spume, are cast
mightily upon one another, until they
rattle like the fetters of giants captive.
Behind them lie Northam Burrows, broad,
smiling expanses clothed with coarse
grass, and delightful to the British golfer,
who there amuses himself religiously,
quite as the Armada captains played at
skittles on the Hoe. Is it beyond possibility that, in our own "empty day,"
some game of golf may be historic?

When and where shall the pilgrim
content himself? Shall he follow the
uttermost traces of those he would fain
have known, and, knowing, offered reverence, even when the present fails to
copy fair the past? If he elect to do so,
then may he seek Freshwater at Clovelly,
where "Irish ffoxe came out of rocks,"
to lose his brush of self-sufficiency, de-
spoiled by giant Amyas ; yet here he will
find but slender trickling of the stream
of clear water, and slight reminder of
such shy quarry, so peaceful is the scene.
He may religiously visit Marsland Mouth,
where lived Lucy Passmore, the "white
witch," to find it a Devonshire combe,
full of every-day contentment ; or he may

traverse Dartmoor, and put the finger of
fancy on the very spot where Salvation
Yeo slew the king of the Gubbings.
Time and enthusiasm must direct him,
but he can scarcely be disappointed in
any Devonian quest, even where he looks
for castle or hovel, and finds not one
stone left upon another; for always and
everywhere are the changeful skies,
warm cliffs, and smiling or tempestuous
sea; everywhere his hope will be set in
the gold of trefoil or the rose of heather.
Devonshire herself has not waxed old
nor faded, and in holding her warm hand
and gazing into her true eyes he may
comfort himself with the certainty that
even so was she in those yesterdays
made for the building of great epics.

IT was during my first summer's travel in Great Britain, now sojourning in hotels where milk was cream and the butter overlaid with gold, and again purringly content in the humblest of lodgings, that I chanced, at Ilfracombe, to secure a bedroom over a dairyman's shop. The finger of fate was in this; for, passing through the shop in search of adventure without, I espied near the doorway a large wooden box marked distinctly "Ridd." To see was figuratively to pounce upon this autographic trace of friend and hero.

"Now, who is Ridd?" quoth I, pointing a dramatic finger at the legend.

"John Ridd, miss?" quaked the shopman, consciously innocent and yet alarmed, viewing the box as it might be a forerunner of November Fifth. "He sends it in full of eggs, miss; and it goes back to him for more."

"But who is John Ridd? Is he a giant? Does he dearly love collops of venison? Did he marry"—

"Bless you, miss!" interrupted my shopman, "all amort:" "he's a dairy-man; but he's nowise remarkable."

This was the first faint footprint of Lorna's John on Devonshire sand: and it greatly inflamed the mind with desire of an extended pilgrimage, wherein Lynton, famed among the jewels of Devon, should be the initial point. Possibly the enthusiast who works by rule and compass would have traced the honest yeoman's career, from its beginning at Blundell School across the moor to Plover's Barrows (even, with painstaking exactitude, locating the Dulverton pump, where he dodged a kiss), thence to his meeting with Lorna, and so on to London Town; but something must at times be sacrificed to the common-sense of travel, and thus it was that we made our path in a measure straight.

Lynton has been a thousand times lauded in breathless interjections, by sounding paragraphs; but it remains the despair of word-imagery. The town is builded upon a wood-covered height, flanked behind by rolling tors, unlimited even by the far distance; and four hundred feet below, approached either by

the lift or a steep, winding track, lies the
little harbor of Lynmouth, cherisher of
the noisy Lyn stream running thereby
and clamoring for the sea.   More like
far-famed Clovelly than any sister town,
Lynmouth has chosen foothold in a cleft
of mighty crags. Majestically they tower
above her, while she broods in peace at
the water gate, guarded in friendly fashion by a quaint Rhenish tower, erected
solely for the delight of artistic eyes.
At a distance of something more than
a mile from Lynton is the Valley of
Rocks, to be approached, if the traveler
is truly wise, only by the cliff walk, — a
footpath cut in the living rock and, faithfully rendered by its name, on the very
face of the cliff.   An enchanted way, it
leads on and on, through almost impossible glories of color and light.   Below,
a sheer descent to the sea, stretches the
cliff. Above, also, it towers inaccessible,
carpeted everywhere with a wondrous
richness of growth.   Heather smiles in
roseate purple, gorse glows resplendent,
and a certain nodding fairy bell intensi-
fies the upper blue. At the right, looking
Lynmouth way, a huge cliff or foreland
sweeps into the sea, "one entire and

perfect chrysolite" in gemlike coloring.
Rich browns shade into purple and rose-
red; and, at those gala moments when
the sunset glory is supreme, the bare
rock throbs and palpitates in almost
breathing beauty. On one late afternoon,
marked forever by a red letter in the
missal of the year, the sky was as a shell,
pink-tinted, lustrous. The sea snatched
its hues, and threw them back in shim-
mering splendor. The great cliff shone
in glory; and the watcher, poised upon
his meagre eyrie, might almost forget
the ground above and beneath, and
imagine himself some happy dweller in
the air, nourished by light and breathing only color. Following this heavenly
way along the curving cliff, the traveler
suddenly turns a corner, and enters the
valley itself. At first, remembering the
stupendous descriptions hung upon its
fame, he is disappointed; but gradually
the true grandeur of the rocky waste
insists upon its own significance. A
valley of some extent, flanked by hills
and to-day traversed by a road, it is
green with bracken and sterile under
stone. Everywhere obtrudes the unyielding rock, in bits fit for a giant's

missile, in massive and uncouth formation, like chaotic dwellings. Two such
rocky citadels, grotesque, tremendous,
attract and hold the eye. These are
Castle Rock and the Devil's Cheese-ring
(the latter word, according to some, sig-
nifying cheese-knife or scoop). Tradition
still declares that in this eerie spot the
witch, Mabel Durham, or, as the name
was corrupted, Mother Melldrum, had
her abode, or possibly her rendezvous;
and thither came John Ridd to seek her.
Wise Mother Melldrum! She knew the
full value of scene-setting and accessories.
Even the valiant John found himself
depressed by the gloom of her surroundings, though he had previously considered the place "nothing to frighten
anybody, unless he had lived in a gal-
lipot." His nerves were as the bass
string, and not the treble; but among the
suppliants for her uncanny aid there
must have been those who here quivered
and quaked in awe of the sorcerer Nature,
if not the human witch.

To extend one's walk along the valley
and through the hospitable gate of Lee
Abbey is to turn a page of romantic history. This estate was some time the

residence of the De Whichehalse family,
Flemish refugees, whose line ended in
revolt against the English crown. One
spot in the grounds furnishes the initial
note to this tragic history, — a cliff overhanging the shore, and still known as
Jennifred's Leap. Jennifred, according
to the story, was beloved and deserted
by Lord Auberley ; and, like Ophelia, she
could not survive the outrage of her
maiden dream. One night she wandered
away from the house, and next morning
had not returned. Search waxed hot
and frantic ; and at length they found
her, happily dead, at the foot of the cliff
where she had cast herself in heroic despair. Her father sought King James for
justice against the recreant lover ; but
Auberley stood high in court favor, and
the royal coward declared his inability to
judge between them. Then came Monmouth's Rebellion ; and De Whichehalse, burning for revenge, repudiated
the royal party, and sought the woman-
slayer in the ranks of its army, met him
face to face, and struck him dead. The
battle of Sedgemoor followed ; and De
Whichehalse, like others of the defeated,
attempted flight to Holland, whereupon

the winds swept down upon him and the
sea rose, quenching his stormy life and
passions forever. But the lover of that
ideal which is forever satisfying, though
the actual betray, will scarcely waste
thought upon this righteous maid-aven-
ger. Rather will he choose to smile over
the memory of that Marwood de Whichehalse who kissed pretty Annie at the
door, and in payment for his whistle was
so sturdily clouted by the giant John.

When John Fry and his valiant little
charge made their way across Exmoor,
from Tiverton to Oare, they halted at
Dulverton ; and there it was that the immortal "farm-hand" demanded "Hot
mootton pasty for twoo trarv'lers, at
number vaive, in vaive minutes!" The
coach road from Lynton thither is characteristic and satisfying ; for on either
side lies the moor, barren, brown, crack-
ling with coarse grass diversified by
patches of heather, "the green of bracken,
the red of whortleberry," and tenanted,
as of old, by ponies and red deer. It is
like Dartmoor as one sister resembles another, and yet strangely individual and
different. Dartmoor is broken by abrupt
hills and gigantic rocky remains: Ex-

moor sweeps away in rolling billows. In
the deep glens at the foot of these enor-
mous earth-ridges hasten clear streams
of varying size, but all swarming with
fish; for the moor is the "mother of
manie rivers." Over the sides of the
ridges themselves trickle swifter rills, in
goyals or gullies, to join the torrent below,— in winter a torrent, indeed; for
then such mountain waters throw aside
the decorum of habit, and swollen by the
early rains leap forth, destructive and
dauntless, to meet the sea. But in the
centre of the great tract, peopled everywhere by thousands of sheep, lie its
monotony and dreariness of waste moorland. It is when they approach the sea
that the great downs become majestic
and truly satisfying. Then they drop
suddenly hundreds of feet, cleft perhaps
by a romantic fissure, where sweeps some
rushing streamlet, foam-fringed and vo-
cal. Here and there are bogs, but alas
for the partisan who would fain shudder
over the bones of Carver Doone bleaching
below the ooze! Not one, says a cool and
unsympathetic authority, is dangerous.

"It always rains on Exmoor," runs
a proverb; and the couplet defining

Dunkery's barometric qualification, announces with the eccentric rhyming of a weather distich, —

> "When Dunkery's top cannot be seen,
>   Horner will have a flooded stream."

Clouds are the hourly attendants of an Exmoor sky; but, when they lower on Dunkery, then the rain may be said to have given official warning of its approach. To climb this beacon hill without a guide is to suffer some diminution of spiritual vainglory, unless, indeed, the gods go with you every step. The pleasantest footway from Porlock leads through the valley of the Horner, where that gurgling, shouting, utterly irresponsible water creature goes tumbling along over stone and shallow, slapping his sides, joking, singing, waking the valley to a madness of mirth. The air there is dark with "green things growing." You can scarcely make your way for love of the thickening leaves on either hand. Everywhere is the beauty woven out of ferns and brawling waters. Crossing the stream is by a foot-bridge made of one timber and a narrow hand-rail. Then you begin climbing, and perhaps like us find yourself, quite out of breath and be-

wildered, in an upland open, apparently
on the way to nowhere. In better
company than the king of France, we
marched down again, mounted another
height and knew only that Exmoor was
about us and that we were plainly lost.
I have little remembrance of that day,
save that it was full of hot sun and
winy airs; that somehow the sound of
an axe led us into a wood, where the
chopper, surprised at visitors in his sleep-
ing world, directed us profusely. All
his conflicting testimony ended to the
tune of: "and that will be Dunkery,
and you'll know it by the b'acon."
Then, obedient, we struck into a way
across the moor. The road rose and
sank with the billowing hills. A little
hamlet glanced out now and then, far
away in a dream. The sky smiled bril-
liantly without a cloud, and scanning it
for the beacon, my eyes looked always
across a black bar where the bright
horizon line had struck them. The hills
were alike, delusive in their sameness.
At length one waving outline seemed to
be broken by a knot, a flaw. Surely the
beacon! No path pointed thither, and
we struck into wild land where the

heather was knee-deep, husky to the ear.
When one of us lay down to rest, the
warm scrubby growth closed over her ;
and the other, looking back, saw only
the sky, the rolling slopes, the few nib-
bling sheep, and drank of wonder, finding herself alone on this great ball, the
earth. The soul must be hide-bound
indeed, if in such space she will not
grow.

At last we were there, — on Dunkery,
with her distinguishing cairn, her vantage
over purpling wastes and love-looks at
the ample sky, and we went back again
through the heather. There were seven
hours of it in all before home and rest :
seven hours without food. But we had
eaten the air and thriven mightily.

From Lynton to Simonsbath (still on
the way to Dulverton) the road affords
you truly typical Exmoor scenery, —
bare, waste, and desolate. This is the
county of the red deer, where he is yet
hunted with the madness of enthusiasm
described by Kingsley and Whyte-Mel-
ville ; and the knowing tourist will scan
the far sinuous horizon for one glimpse
of a delicate antlered head. Vain desire !
He is lying somewhere in covert, de-

veloping his tactics for the next meet. Then perchance he will slink into the lair of a young stag, and send him forth with a cruel push of resistless horns, to draw the sportsman's eye. If that avail not, he will seek some still watercourse, and there cool him in the stream before picking his dainty way over moss and pebble, — every step a move in the game of outwitting the hounds, his enemies to the death. But lay it not to heart, dear pilgrim, if the only four-footed beasties you find on Exmoor are ponies cropping the homely herbage : the deer are meat for our masters.

Simonsbath is dignified by the usual quota of legend, though it happens to be of a rather fragmentary and commonplace nature. The name is taken, says one tale, from a deep pool in the Barle, where Simon, an Exmoor outlaw of some unknown period, was accustomed to bathe. Another folk tradition connects it with King Sigmund, the dragon-slayer. But sufficient be it for us to remember, when we draw up in front of the William Rufus, a tavern in good and respectable standing to-day as it was two centuries ago, that this was the scene of one mar-

velous escape ascribed to Tom Faggus.
Here was he one night reveling when
the authorities suddenly pounced upon
him, — only to be outwitted, however;
for Tom had but to leap on his half-
human strawberry mare and ride away.
J. Ll. W. Page, lover of the moors of
Exe and Dart, quotes, for the benefit of
the imaginative, the tradition that the
bog known as Claren Rocks, not far
from Simonsbath, was the instrument of
Carver Doone's tragic ending; but, as he
justly adds, a certain wet patch upon the
side of Dunkery may, with equal likeli-
hood, receive the popular vote. As in
more vital matters, doctors disagree;
and the hoarder of such uncertain detail
might as well look about him, within the
proper radius, and fix upon any bog even
approximately answering the require-
ments of fancy. The verdict has been
given, the case dismissed : circumstantial evidence can do no harm. Beyond
Simonsbath, the road becomes somewhat
tame, in comparison with its previous
mood; and at Dulverton itself, entered
by a street so narrow that the houses
seem inhospitably to elbow the passing
coach, there is scanty interest for anti-

quary and for "tripper." You may climb
the hill behind the church and overlook
the valley of the Barle, or you may drive
through the wooded luxury of Earl Car-
narvon's park; but it must be confessed
that the chief glory of the place lies now
in the memory of John Fry's " hot mootton pasty." Not far away are the Tor
Steps, near which Mother Melldrum set
up her summer residence. A rude bridge
made of stone slabs, placed upon piers
and guiltless of cement, — this, it seems,
was built by the devil for his own ex-
clusive use. He threatened destruction
to the first living creature crossing it,
whereupon the parson, who was amazingly clever in those days at outwitting
the fiend, broke the spell by sending
over "a harmless necessary cat." Pussy
was torn piecemeal ; and then the parson
himself crossed in safety, billingsgating
the devil as he went. The dialogue on
this memorable occasion must have been
of the *tu quoque* order, inasmuch as the
parson was called a "black crow," and
avenged himself for the indignity offered
his garb by retorting that he was "no
blacker than the devil." Shrewd in tactics, it is evident that this good gentle-

man was yet a dullard at repartee, else would he have chosen some more biting rejoinder than " You're another ! "

Let no one contemplating the coaching trip to Dulverton be deceived by the announcement that the Doone Valley is among the attractions of the route; for this beguiling statement merely indicates that the driver, at a certain stage of the trip, will point vaguely into the purple distance, and remark that the Doone Valley is "there." The greedy traveler, however, hardly needs to be told that he should take a carriage at Lynmouth, and make a canny bargain for a drive to the valley itself, — preferably by the Countisbury Road, to return by way of Watersmeet, where the Combe Park and Farley Waters join the East Lyn with many sparkles of delight at the meeting and much pomp of fern-embroidered garment. (This, however, applies only to those who, like the Queen of Spain, have no legs. A walker will make it a day's excursion, thanking his luck for the chance.) Up and out into the clear air of heaven leads the Countisbury Road, skirting the very brow of sheer cliffs on one side, and

smiled on by Exmoor from the inland
distance. The blue sea and the shadowy coast of Wales are the wayfarer's
treasure-trove. Every breath is exhil-
arating, sweet, instinct with beauty.
Presently the road inclines downward
and toward the right ; and Devonshire
is left behind for the goodly county of
Somerset, claimant also for the parentage of the redoubtable John. ("Zummerzett thou bee'st, Jan Ridd," said the
popular voice on that side the line, "and
Zummerzett thou shalt be.") And before reaching the goal of his desire, it
shall befall the traveler to seek out Oare
church, a tiny building with nave and
chancel all complete, like a temple of
Lilliput Land ; and there I wish him
not too exhaustive a knowledge of what
he is to find. For I, in entering, expected
merely to drink from the cup of sweet
memories, reflecting, " Here stood John
with his Lorna when Carver's shot came
crashing in, charged with death to one
and madness for her lover ; " but pure
surprise chased such sentimental musing from the field. Stepping within
the nave, the previously uninstructed is
amazed at certain tablets on the north

wall ; for these perpetuate the memory of the Snowe family, to which Blackmore has vouchsafed a long-lasting tenure of life, and one of them is even adorned by the name of Farmer Nicholas himself, though of another generation than John's old neighbor. The Snowes, so saith the chronicler, are worthy yeomen who have held land in this region since the days of Alfred ; and this enduring brass doth so plainly resurrect them before the eye that one is tempted to subscribe then and there to a sober belief in all Blackmore's broidery of fact, asserting, "The bricks are alive at this day to testify it."

Beyond Oare, the road is less diversified ; and at Malmsmead, a collection of two or three houses devoted, as by an irrevocable vow, to the upholding of Doone legends, you may take an Exmoor pony and ride along a sweetly sylvan path into the true valley. And here, at whatever season you go, so that green boughs be welcoming, it shall seem "the boyhood of the year ;" for everywhere is budding or expanded growth, under dappling of shadow and flickering of light. After Blackmore's pæan, all that one can

say of the Doone Valley rings of bathos,
the more lukewarm in proportion to its
truth. For here, indeed, is the water-
slide, a rocky incline covered by a thin
streamlet, amicably flowing to meet the
Bagworthy Water ; but it is by no means
a way perilous, and its ascent need not
have tired little John's stout muscles
so sorely. The valley itself, broken by
the desolate foundations of a few tiny
huts, is hemmed in by moorland hills ;
but, compared with a score of Exmoor's
chasms and retreats, it is as Leah to
Rachel. We are in the home of the
Doones ; and very fair it is, with the
summer sky above us and the whispering
leaves at hand. But the magic picture
of our search we shall by no means find,
save between the covers of Blackmore's
book wonderful. Learn, however, the
sequel : forget not the epilogue ! For,
when one has turned his back on this
disappointing spot and taken his homeward road, he cannot forbear exclama-
tion, at more points than one, over the
actual valley of his dreams. For the
reality of that word-picture exists, though
not where tradition has placed it. Here
are steep inclines, hundreds of feet high,

down which even the anguished red deer
dare not hurl himself in his extremity
of flight.   Here are inaccessible gullies,
foaming water, and fern-clad hollow.
And thus it is that he who truly seeks
will find, even though the prize be long
deferred.

There are few places in whose records
I take more delight than in those of
Tiverton and her Blundell School. Who
that has the heart of youth does not recall, with a responsive thrill, John Ridd's
tale of the Blundell boys' heaven-sent
holiday?   For "in the very front of the
gate, just without the archway, where the
ground is paved most handsomely, you
may see in copy-letters done a great
P. B. of white pebbles. Now it is the
custom and the law that, when the invading waters, either fluxing along the
wall from below the road-bridge or pour-
ing sharply across the meadows from
a cut called 'Owen's ditch,'— and I
myself have seen it come both ways,—
upon the very instant when the waxing
element lips though it be but a single
pebble of the founder's letters, it is in
the license of any boy, so ever small and
undoctrined, to rush into the great

school-rooms, where a score of masters sit heavily, and scream at the top of his voice, ' P. B. ! '

"Then, with a yell, the boys leap up or break away from their standing. They toss their caps to the black-beamed roof, and haply the very books after them; and the great boys vex no more the small ones, and the small boys stick up to the great ones. One with another, hard they go, to see the gain of the waters, . . . and are prone to kick the day-boys out, with words of scanty compliment. Then the masters look at one another, having no class to look to, and (boys being no more left to watch) in a manner they put their mouths up. With a spirited bang they close their books, and make invitation, the one to the other, for pipes .and foreign cordials, recommending the chance of the time and the comfort away from cold water."

Peter Blundell, the founder of the school, was, according to good John Prince, "at first a very Poor Lad of Tiverton; who, for a little Support, went Errands for the Carriers that came to that Town, and was Tractable in looking after their Horses and doing little Ser-

vices for them, as they gave him Orders.
By degrees, in such means, he got a
little Money, of which he was very Provi-
dent and Careful ; and bought therewith
a kersey, which a Carrier was so kind as
to carry to London, gratis, and to make
him the Advantage of the Return. Having done so for some time, he at length
got kersies enough to Lade an Horse,
and went up to London with it humbly :
Where being found very Diligent and
Industrious, he was received into good
Imployment by those who managed there
the Kersey Trade (for which Tiverton
was then very famous), and he continued
therein, until he was Rich enough to set
up the Calling of making Kersies for
himself. . . . He came at last to a vast
and large Estate ; whereby he was en-
abled to do such noble Benefactions, and
bestow such large Legacies as he did."

The school itself is painstakingly described by this ever-delightful chronicler :

"This House stands at the East end
of the Town, a very tall and spacious
Structure, built something like the Col-
lege-Halls in the Universities, with a fair
Cupulo in the middle. The Pile contains
one School for the Master, and another

for the Usher, only an entry between them; both, by his Direction, One hundred Foot long, and four and twenty broad; well wainscoted and Boarded. Close adjoyning to which, is a very large House for the Master, and another convenient one for the Usher: with very good Orchards, Gardens, and Out-Lots, belonging to it.

"Before the School-House is a large spacious Green-Court, in Figure a Quadrangle, in Continent one Acre of Ground, at the enterance in from the Street. All enclosed with an high and stately Wall, coped with yellow Purbeck-Stone, very handsome to behold. It hath a fair Gate at the Entry into it, over which is this Inscription, cut in Stone, now rendered by Time and Weather almost illegible.

"'This Free Grammar-School was Founded at the only Cost and Charge of Mr. Peter Blundell of this Town, some times Clothier.'"

Outwardly, alas! the Blundell's of "Lorna Doone" is no more. In 1880 new buildings were erected, nearly a mile away, and the old ones, sold under certain conditions, were converted into dwelling-houses. Thus it is that Tiverton is

sadly disappointing to a visitor weak in
the memory. These facts I knew, but
somehow they slipped my mind, as pins
run into cracks, and when I passed that
"high and stately Wall," on my way from
the station, I smiled at the "fair Gate"
leading therein, and was content, knowing how securely tradition rested there
and would rest. But next day's sun,
according to immemorial right, dispelled
my fancy. I might peep within at walls
and velvet sward, but the spirit of old
Blundell's had fled. I lingered, scowling
at the spirit of change, and then took my
dusty way up the hill, to glare at the
prosperous modern buildings of new old
Blundell's and greet the transplanted
P. B. loyally holding place at the entrance
gates.

"Never again, I fear," writes a master
of the school, "can the waters of the
Lowman hope to cover these honored
initials, — at least, in the ordinary course
of things ; and I can hardly contemplate
the possibility that the 'license of any
boy' should extend to the length of
'rushing into the school-room, crying P.
B.' Such a course of action would not
recommend itself to any Blundellian of

the present day as likely to obtain a holiday for the school.   This luxury is rarely granted nowadays."

Readers of Blackmore, himself a Blundellian, will remember his account of the perpetual feuds between boarders and day-boys : —

"For it had been long fixed among us, who were of the house and chambers, that these same day-boys were all 'caddes,' as we had discovered to call it, because they paid no groat for their schooling and brought their own commons with them.   In consumption of these we would help them, for our fare in hall fed appetite ; and, while we ate their victuals, we allowed them freely to talk to us.   Nevertheless, we could not feel, when all the victuals were gone, but that these boys required kicking from the premises of Blundell."

But at length did "the whirligig of time," consonant to eternal word, "bring in his revenges."   For in 1846, according to F. H. Snell, a former Blundell scholar at Oxford, a dispute, which had long been pending between the Feoffees of the school and the inhabitants of Tiverton, terminated in the victory of the

latter. These worthy citizens complained
that, whereas the Blundell benefaction
had been intended primarily for Tiverton boys, its privileges were eaten up by
boarders, who not only absorbed most of
the scholarship fund, but despised and
harried the native students (or "cads!").
Proceedings ran a long and tortuous
course; but the final decision given by
the Vice-Chancellor was that "neither
the Master nor the Usher of the said
School ought to receive any payments
from or in respect of any of the boys
educated in the said School, or ought
to take any boarder; and that none but
boys educated as Free Scholars, *videli-
cet*, Scholars free of expense in the said
School, . . . ought to be eligible to the
said Scholarships and Exhibitions." Then
followed a dreary period; for the imme-
diate effect of the decree had been to
sweep away at least half the number of
pupils, and the provisions for teaching
the remainder were by no means satis-
factory. However, matters slowly read-
justed themselves; and at the present
writing, Blundell's boasts a goodly roll of
boarders and day scholars, who, if they
do loyally continue the ancient feud,

doubtless proceed in the scientific fashion observed by John Ridd and Robin Snell.

Tiverton herself is all lovable in her assured and not too flaunting prosperity, and the spirit of her people is worthy of the county; for nowhere in England do you find truer and more unfailing courtesy than in Devon. It was in Tiverton that one short day gave me a round of social delights, chiefly at almshouses, where dear old women potter about their tiny quarters in a flutter of hospitality, bringing out their last treasures of china for your sake — ancient teapots and copper-lustre half-pints which they lingeringly agree to sell, but with such evident agony of soul that you incontinently refuse the bargain and flee from temptation. Yet it is to be hoped that here the nimble shilling leaps from your purse into some eager, wrinkled hand; for a shilling buys much tea.

The White Horse Inn, where "girt Jan" rested after his victory over Robin, still exists in Gold Street, but inevitable joy thereat is tempered by the fact that the "souls of John and Joan Greenway," mentioned tenderly by Blackmore, could scarcely have found there a congenial resting-place; for they have long since disappeared. They may, however, be heard of across the road, at Greenway's Chapel or Almshouses, which are still in being, and have not been diverted from their original uses.

There is, perhaps, no more pathetic record contained in those letters graven by men who would fain assure to themselves a brief immortality than that set down by John and Joan Greenway, who seemed strangely timorous as to their reception in the next world and extravagantly desirous of establishing some sort of lien on the kindly feeling of this. John Greenway, though "of mean parentage," grew "vastly Rich," and in the early part of the sixteenth century founded an almshouse for a limited number of poor men, endowing them with a small weekly revenue. He added a chapel to the church; and there, according to Prince, "in a spacious Vault, . . . under a large Stone, lieth this John Greenway and his Wife Joan; on which the Figures of them both, curiously done in Brass, are fixed: round the Edges goes a Fillet of Brass, having their Epitaph engraven on it, in old Characters, now partly obliterated: what remains legible here follows:—

"'Of your Charite prey for the Souls
of John and Joan Greenway his Wife
which Died . . . and for their
Faders and Moders, and for their Friends
and their Lovers. On them Jesu
have Mercy. Amen.'

"Out of the mouth of John Greenway
proceeds a Label of Brass, on which are
these Words,

"'O! then to thee we pray,
Have mercy of John Greenway.'"

His wife had, in her own name, the
benefit of the same pious wish. And,
though these labels have long since been
torn away, the chapel, even after sad
experience of the vandalism known as
restoration, bears continually reiterated
petitions for John Greenway's heavenly
welfare, and that of his spouse. On the
exterior are inscribed the mottoes :—

"God sped J. G."

"Of your charitie pray for the Souls
of John Greenway and his wife."

"Oh Lord all way grant to John
Grenway good fōtūe and grace
and In heaven a place!"

Everywhere was repeated that pathetic injunction, like a cry from some far and solitary land : — "Pray for John Greenway!" Alas, poor ghost! Did he find this earth and his foothold at Tiverton too goodly to be relinquished, or was he by nature a distrustful soul, who shrank from those new worlds which the poorest of us must conquer? Is he, indeed, at rest, or doth his immortal part still protest against its progress to another star? Pray for his soul!

And in this relic-hunting of the Doones, what must be the conclusion of the whole matter? That a band of outlaws two hundred years ago built their huts in an isolated valley, and lived there a life of rapine and shame; that John Ridd, the champion wrestler and eater of beef, is hotly believed in by the sons of Devon, to whom legend has been handed down like family jewels; and that Tom Faggus and his strawberry mare, and even Betty Muxworthy, are articles of local faith. But what are these but the dry bones of belief? Supreme and vital walks the glowing truth that a beautiful book was born of their ashes, and that its fame shall be ever-living.

ALL over England are scattered the footprints of King Arthur, legendary hero and crown of chivalry. His prowess is chanted by mountain streamlets, and lowland rushes whisper his name. Cornwall wears the renown of his birth, and most appropriately; for it is the county of giants and fairies, of saint and mythic hero. To this day, it has preserved more of its old-time character than any other corner in England; and the traveler need spur his imagination but slightly to feel, on entering its borders, that he has reached the land of ancient custom and romance. Varied and seemingly inexhaustible are its antiquities. Here are barrows, cromlechs, stone-rings, and ruined fortifications, to occupy the speculations of Dryasdust. Neither need the romantic wanderer depart unfed, for in this still, secluded spot awaiteth him many a delightsome morsel. By night, he may hear the wailing of Tregeagle, spirit haunted by demons, and doomed to ex-

piate a wicked life by perpetual toil at
impossible tasks; or he may steep his
soul in that solace which is a sort of in-
tellectual nicotine by turning the pages
of legend, from the story of the Giant
Cormoran to that of Britain's hero-king.

Cornwall, like most regions diversified
by a huge and rocky formation, was once,
according to the popular belief, overrun
with giants, from whom it was delivered
by that noble Jack, son of a wealthy
farmer near Land's End, who first earned
his sobriquet of "Giant Killer" by slay-
ing the terrible Cormoran, builder and
lord of Saint Michael's Mount. In Cornwall lived also the Giant Bolster. He
made nothing of compassing six miles
at a stride, and yet was overtaken by
fate in the person of Saint Agnes, whom
he so persecuted with offers of affection
that she was compelled, in self-defense,
to entrap him into an amiable suicide.
All over the duchy are scattered names
recalling that age of wonder. There are
giants' cradles, graves, pulpits, spoons,
and bowls; and though one legend declares that the devil dare not enter Cornwall for fear of being made into a pie
(for at least three hundred varieties of

pasty have flourished at one time or another on the west Tamar side), still he
has served as sponsor for many a natural
oddity. Indeed, as one antiquary declares, in the eastern part of Cornwall
every phenomenon out of the common
course is referred to King Arthur; in
the west, to giants or the devil. The
subject of Cornish pies, however, is one
which is not to be lightly dismissed.
The most casual consideration of it puts
forever to flight certain dogmatic asser-
tions regarding the lack of variety in
English cooking. Cornwall has pies of
beef, duck, and conger-eel, lammy pies,
concocted of the succulent kid : and, as
hath been said, star-gazing pies, made
of pilchards. In short, their name is
that of a legion alarming to the con-
servative foreigner. Only a temperate
mind may choose among such pretty
dishes "to set before the king." To-
day, pilchard fishing is the great industry of the coast, furnishing a wealth not
to be despised beside that which once
lay in tin and copper. The local tin
mines are almost exhausted, — scarcely
a subject for wonder when we consider
that before the Christian era they were

supplying Greek, Roman, and Phœnician merchants with metal loaded at the port Iktis, now Saint Michael's Mount. This, therefore, is an old, old civilization; and here, to a very late date, have been preserved the customs of a sparsely chronicled time. Droll-tellers, a species of wandering minstrel, went formerly from house to house, gladly welcomed and hospitably entertained, to sing folk ballads and repeat old tales. Even as late as the first part of the present century two such venders of "drolls," or tales of marvel and delight, were still alive. This was a quaint and simple people, albeit somewhat chary of communicating its old-time legends to alien folk. The terms "uncle" and "aunt" were freely interchanged among them in token of respect and affection; and thus did the Virgin Mary come to be tenderly spoken of as *Modryb Marya*, "Aunt Mary." One subject, however, to this day rouses them to wrath, — the comparison of their clotted cream with the cream of Devon. "Ah, you can't make Cornish cream anywhere else!" said a wise old woman. "It takes Cornish cows." That I firmly believe; and yet, when in Devonshire, I am convinced of the paramount excellence of Devonshire cows. There is no such cream as the Cornish cream save in Devonshire, and none like the Devon cream except in Cornwall.

The coast of Cornwall is rock-bound, full of terrible crags, of sounding caves, and beaten upon by mighty surges. Yet, inland from its rocky strongholds, how the earth smiles in leaf and bloom! In its valleys, on the south coast, blossoms a tropical wealth of flowers, quite amazing in a country of England's latitude. Fuchsias, roof-high, adorn the cottage fronts; scarlet geraniums and roses clamber to their very caves. Near the Lizard grows the wonderful Cornish heath, found nowhere else but in Portugal,— delicate and gracious sojourner from a warmer clime. In the sweet freshness of the sea winds every petal assumes a brilliancy of tint unknown farther inland. The heather is rosier, the gorse has a more golden glow, foxgloves are reddened by a lustier current. Over the headlands, to the very beginning of their rocky defenses, grows the pink thrift, and, painting the rocks themselves, creeps a golden lichen. Its domestic features have a character all their own. Tiny stone cottages, whitewashed and roofed with slate, stand in clustering sociability, each little hamlet with its gray stone church, crouching low to avoid the winds, and with a square tower often high enough for a beacon. Many a village is under saintly patronage, like Saint Ives, Saint Sennen, or Saint Just. Saints were plentiful here; and, indeed, one authority declares that in the Cornish folk-lore it is difficult to distinguish their deeds from those of the giants.

In seeking this land of eld, my first thought was of that heroic king — giant among his contemporaries — who set his seal upon the sixth century, and whose name has passed into the literature of France and Italy, to creep back from the former into his own land by means of Sir Thomas Malory's pen and Caxton's press.

A public coach furnishes conveyance from Newquay to Tintagel, by way of Boscastle, a little town rich in a store of antiquarian memories, and adorned by fine headlands and a quaint harbor, certain to delight the artistic eye. To those unfamiliar with the face of this particular

region, the road reads a pleasing pre-
lude to the peculiar beauties of Cornwall.
It is monotonous compared with certain
drives along the Devon coast; yet its
quiet charm is such as one would be
loath to miss. This is a country of ridgy,
wind-swept hills, garnished by a scanty
tree growth, and looking down into
sweet valleys, where, especially in the
south, lies all its luxuriance of growth
and bloom. The Cornish hedges are lit-
erally banks, made of earth and stone,
some of them ten feet high, and often
with a surface of two feet at the top,
either planted with shrubs or left bare for
a footpath. In this cementing earth has
taken root all manner of creeping things
and blossoming life. Besides the may
and honeysuckle, I have gathered pim-
pernel, a royal yellow trefoil, thyme, and
foxglove from their crannies; but chiefly
are they overspread with a rich mantle
of heath. On that day when we drove to
Tintagel, perhaps over the ground where
Iseult rode, with hawk on wrist, or Tristram carolled, — sad of name, but gay in
Gallic grace, — the sky was full of windy
clouds and the air passing chill. Yet the
whole landscape was lightened and glo-

rified by these hedges of rose-purple heather, like broad, rich lines of crimson laid on by a daring and prodigal brush. Past quarries and great refuse-heaps of slate the road leads down and then up again into the little town of Tintagel, or Trevena, where stood twin castles on headland and promontory, scene of the siege of Gorlois, Duke of Tintagel, by Uther Pendragon, and undoubtedly the place of Arthur's birth. Gorlois, with his wife, the fair Igraine, had visited the court; and there King Uther turned on the lady such eyes of favor that she besought her husband to take her home to Cornwall. Vain flight! for Uther Pendragon followed, killed the duke, and wedded the lady. From the little village of Trevena a path winds seaward, where a bold promontory juts out into the deep. This was once connected with the mainland by a drawbridge; and twin fortifications stood on either side, hand thus clasped in hand, until the falling of a crag had made the promontory into an island. It may be reached, however, by a little bridge, and over a seemingly perilous way, from stone to stone, to a steep and winding path over the very face of

the cliff.   Midway, the climber is con-
fronted by a heavy wooden door; but,
when this swings back, obedient to the
key with which he is entrusted, he enters what was undoubtedly an actual British stronghold, if not that of Tintagel's
duke.   Within, flocks of sheep are peacefully feeding among the huge, disordered
blocks of stone, once firm in towered
strength above the changing tide.   Here
are the foundations of chapel and castle,
a possible altar-stone, and the signs of
a burial-place.   Tintagel's coast is grim
and rough as mountain fastnesses.   Out
into the sea stride its rocks like conquering giants, and the sea dashes at
them, disdainful, mighty, but helpless.
How must Igraine have trembled when,
shut up for safety while her lord occupied the castle of Terrabil, she heard
the waves moan and the wind howl, and
knew — for in that childlike age such
things were known — that destiny had
her in toils from which there was no es-
caping !   A little cove, or landing-place,
makes its way between the two headlands ; and here perhaps the babe Arthur
was washed up to the hands of Merlin.
Or, if that tale be but idly told, Arthur

was assuredly born of Igraine in that
very castle, and delivered into the charge
of Sir Ector, waiting for him outside the
postern gate, according to the compact
made by the king with the magician, .
when Merlin procured Uther Pendragon
access to Igraine's favor. At Tintagel
dwelt also those unhappy lovers, play-
things of an unswerving fate, Tristram
and Iseult. Tristram was nephew of
Mark, King of Cornwall. He had been
educated in Brittany, and brought thence
the embroidery of manner for which
France has ever been a nursery. Mark's
ambassador to bring home the fair
Iseult for her crowning, knight and lady,
through the craft of Iseult's maid, drank
a potent love-philter, and thenceforward
loved deathlessly, and to their own un-
doing. Here did Iseult pine and suffer
after their separation, until Tristram,
wedded in Brittany to Iseult of the
White Hands, sent for her, in his mortal illness, to shrive him from sorrow
with her kiss. Over these waves she
sailed ; and there in Brittany, with her
tristful lover, she died.

To catch the spirit of this place, one
must linger long in it, feeding his eye

with the changeful beauty of the sea,
and pondering on the rocky might of
the unyielding shore. It is a coast
whose fist of stone seems to hold se-
crets of the past, of a time of tragic love,
of iron if mistaken resolve and of that
death which leads to deathless fame.
On one bluff, rising sheer and steep
from the water, stands the little church,
neighbored by its quiet graveyard and
approached through the solemn lych-
gate, with its stone slab for supporting
the coffin while the bearers rest. To
climb this height in the late afternoon
and watch the sun until it sinks into
the sea, with all the magnificence of a
changeful but silent pageant, while the
water ceaselessly washes on the crags
below, and death and worship keep ward
behind, is a strangely sweet and solemn
experience. The gulls fly, calling, from
rock to rock, dip their wings and wheel
back again, or rest an instant on the
unquiet deep. At such a moment, why
should not the red-legged chough, in
whose likeness Arthur revisits his native haunts, flit unrecognized by? Skirting the headland at the left of the
church, winding down by zigzagging de-

grees, is a path leading to the slate quarries ; and there all day men are splitting
slate, cutting it into squares and sending it over into the harbor, to be taken
away in boats. There they toil, seemingly on the face of the cliff, in safety,
and yet, to the unaccustomed eye, at almost the perilous height where samphire
gatherers hang. At twilight, however,
they are gone, and the place is still;
only, perhaps, some dark-haired, stalwart
miner comes striding across the height,
to offer you sea-birds' eggs for sale, or
crystals found in the quarried slate, and
known as Cornish diamonds. Then, as
the gray wings of twilight softly settle,
turn homeward by the lowly road sunken
in the valley, past the rectory, embow-
ered in green, and sleep, perhaps murmuring, like Guinevere's little maid, —

"I thank the saints I am not great!"—

that destiny has not for all such store
of tragedy as it brought those childlike,
passionate souls of an earlier day who
dwelt in rock-bound castles, and chal-
lenged fate in the daily struggles of a
tumultuous living.

After the death of Uther Pendragon,
when many mighty lords coveted succes-

sion to the throne, Merlin counseled the
Archbishop of Canterbury to send all
the gentlemen of the realm to London;
and there they found, in the great church
of the city, against the high altar, a stone,
and in its midst a steel anvil. Therein
stuck a fair sword, naked, by the point;
and letters of gold were written about
the sword saying thus: "Whoso pull-
eth out this sword of this stone and anvil is rightwise born King of England."
And many knights essayed the task;
but none but Arthur could pull it out,
"lightly and fiercely." Then arose
much wrangling among the nobles
whether he were a truly begotten son
of Uther Pendragon, so that his corona-
tion was long deferred; but, when at
last it was holden, it was at the city of
Caerleon upon Usk; or, as some say, he
was merely consecrated there, and afterwards crowned at Stonehenge. Caerleon
is a town of indisputable antiquity; but
to-day all it can offer the most enthusiastic pilgrim is a grassy mound, several
acres in circumference, depressed in the
centre, whereon stood Arthur's castle.
The view from the circular grassy ram-
part takes in the placid valley of the Usk,

a muddy little stream, fleeing away to join the Severn. The valley is encircled by hills, and these are flanked by others still higher ; yet the prospect is neither bold nor vast. It seems to mirror the humble beginning of Arthur's supremacy, before he held court at Camelot or at Westminster. At the latter place, it must be remembered, his seat was fixed when Elaine, the "Lily Maid," floated down from Astolat, or Guildford, in Surrey. When he had married Guinevere, daughter of King Leodograunce, he kept his royal state at Camelot ; and, in settling upon the modern equivalent of that enchanted spot, the traveler may please his fancy, if he have not a painfully critical mind, and can be content with what the wise may frown upon. Was it Winchester ? That is a goodly and ancient town ; and, if he choose to wander by the smooth-flowing Itchen, dreaming of souls more heroic than Izaak Walton, who shall blame him ? If he look with reverent eye upon the stone coffin there displayed as Arthur's, shall we pronounce him childishly credulous ? Or, perhaps, with the faith of the tourist in an oft-proven Baedeker, he will assume that Camelot was Camelford, a little town six miles from Trevena, presided over by Row Tor and Brown Willy, the two highest mountains in Cornwall. Not far from Camelford is the stone bridge called "Slaughter Bridge," said to be the scene of Arthur's disastrous defeat. Yet no one need waste over it too deep a sentiment; for antiquaries have declared that the half obliterated inscription on the slab once spanning the stream (and some years ago removed, to be set up in better view) has nothing whatever to do with the British king. Scene of a British fight no doubt it was, but not of Arthur's battle. The most reliable evidence, however, is in favor of Queen's Camel, or South Cadbury, in Somersetshire. There, in the midst of a fertile and diversified country, stands a hill, leveled at the top to form a circular plain, and commanding a right royal view of wood, meadow, and tor beyond. At its feet lie scattered hamlets, humble cottages, each group with its gray, square-towered church, — mild symbol of the peaceful domestic life which slept and ate below that heroic one of court and chivalry. Here Guine-

vere and Launcelot kissed and sighed.
Here did the innocent glow of their first
bond — that of knight and sovereign
lady — deepen into that passion which
was crime.

The scene of Arthur's defeat, —

"that last weird battle in the West," —

has not been determined with absolute
certainty; but the balance of evidence —
swelled, surely, by the voluntary testimony of those who have compared the
poetic values of the region — is in favor
of Salisbury Plain, loneliest land-stretch
imaginable by poet or dreamer.   Exactly what it is which stamps the plain
with eerie awesomeness it would be difficult to say.   Let the wayfarer wind
slowly up and up from spired Salisbury
town, past Old Sarum, and gradually
there falls upon him a certainty that
here is, if not the strength of the hills,
their utter loneliness.   The few dwellings and dotted trees do not in the least
serve to break that sweeping expanse.
The larks run up their ascending scale
of joy from the first low-brooding ground-
notes to ecstatic lyrics, lost in the highest blue; the sun intermittently casts
down a Danaë shower, — yet still is the

place an embodiment of desolation. It is like a formless, monstrous presence, oppressing the soul. It is the sphinx, the very spirit of the desert, but the sphinx become blind and dumb. Crowning the utmost height of the plain are those giant monoliths, the disordered order of Stonehenge, about which clings a legend of Merlin. Not far from here, says tradition, was the scene of a British victory, and, when the Britons proposed commemorating it by a monument, Merlin advised them to take away from a mountain in Ireland the structure called the Giant's Dance, formed of stones stolen by giants from the coast of Africa, and possessing mystical virtues. It was Uther Pendragon who finally conquered Ireland, and sought to remove the stones ; but, finding the task beyond the power of mortal mechanics, he called Merlin to his aid, who speedily accomplished it by magic. There is a certain dramatic satisfaction in imagining the battle here, under the very shadow of the triumphal pile erected by Arthur's fostering magician. Here was commemorated the Briton's triumph — here was a Briton overthrown.

To the east of Stonehenge, in a greenly wooded valley, lies the little town of Amesbury, Almesbury, or Ambrosebury, where Guinevere sought refuge when she "understood that her lord, King Arthur, was slain." This was the scene of her last interview with Sir Launcelot, most moving, in its passionate simplicity, of all the incidents which form this tragic chronicle : —

"And then was Queen Guenever aware of Sir Launcelot as he walked in the cloister ; and when she saw him there, she swooned three times, that all the ladies and gentlewomen had work enough for to hold the queen up. So, when she might speak, she called the ladies and gentlewomen unto her : 'Ye marvel, fair ladies, why I make this cheer. Truly,' said she, 'it is for the sight of yonder knight which is yonder : wherefore, I pray you all to call him unto me.' And when Sir Launcelot was brought unto her, then she said, 'Through this knight and me all the wars were wrought, and the death of the most noble knights of the world ; for through our love that we have loved together is my most noble lord slain.

Therefore, wit thou well, Sir Launcelot, I am set in such a plight to get my soul's health; and yet I trust, through God's grace, that after my death for to have the sight of the blessed face of Jesu Christ, and at the dreadful day of doom to sit on his right side, — for as sinful creatures as ever was I are saints in heaven.

"'Therefore, Sir Launcelot, I require thee, and beseech thee heartily, for all the love that ever was between us two that thou never look me more in the visage: and, furthermore, I command thee, on God's behalf, right straightly that thou forsake my company, and that unto thy kingdom shortly thou return again, and keep well thy realm from war and wreck. For as well as I have loved thee, Sir Launcelot, now mine heart will not once serve me to see thee; for through me and thee are the flower of kings and knights destroyed. Therefore, Sir Launcelot, go thou unto thy realm, and there take thee a wife, and live with her in joy and bliss; and I beseech you heartily pray for me unto our Lord God, that I may amend my misliving.'"

Then like a true knight obedient to

his lady, did Sir Launcelot answer her
that, although he had hoped to carry her
into his own realm and country, since
she would not have it so, he also must
take to prayer and penance while life
should last.

"'Wherefore, madam, I pray you kiss
me once, and nevermore.'

"'Nay,' said the queen, 'that shall I
never do; but abstain you from such
things.' And so they departed; but
there was never so hardhearted a man
but he would have wept to see the sorrow they made, for there was lamenta-
tion as though they had been stung
with spears, and many times they
swooned."

And when Sir Launcelot at length
rode away through the forest, weeping,
he came upon a hermitage and a chapel,
where a little bell was ringing to mass.
He threw away his armor, and knelt to
be assoiled from sin; and there he remained "serving God, day and night,
with prayers and fastings." After six
years there came to him a vision, charg-
ing him to hasten to Almesbury, where
he would find Queen Guinevere dead;
thence should he carry her body, and lay

it beside that of King Arthur. Meantime, the dying queen had learned, also in a vision, that Launcelot had been called to that dolorous task, and it was her prayer, for the two days before her death, that she "might never see Sir Launcelot with her worldly eyes." For the mighty passion of that love had burnt on and on through hours of penance and prayer; it had eaten up the mortal frame, its habitation. Then did Sir Launcelot and seven fellow-monks bear the queen's body to Glastonbury, where she was buried, with dirge and requiem; and there did he speak over her those lofty words, which fitly end the tragic tale : —

"My sorrow may never have an end. For when I remember and call to mind her beauty, her bounty, and her nobleness, that was as well with her king, my Lord Arthur, as with her ; and also when I saw the corpse of that noble king, and noble queen, so lie together in that cold grave made of earth, that sometime was so highly set in most honorable places, truly mine heart would not serve me to sustain my wretched and careful body."

Amesbury was one of the oldest

centres of British civilization, and its monastery — afterwards a convent of Benedictine nuns — doubtless flourished under the protection of Aurelius Ambrosius, the British prince who so long and so successfully defended his country against the Saxons. Past the little town winds Avon's "troutful stream," and a lonely church sits in the hamlet's midst, still solitary, though encompassed by lowly dwellings. This church, however, does not cover the site of the former monastery : that is now included within private grounds, and the stones once forming the walls have hopelessly lost their identity among those of modern buildings. Amesbury, at the present day, seen under a shifting sky, is a still and thoughtful place, bearing ever a haunting suggestion of romance and remembrance.

Tennyson fixes the scene of Arthur's last great struggle in the land of Lyonesse, under the eternal washing of the surge sweeping between Land's End and the Scilly Isles. An almost uninterrupted tradition declares that these islands were once joined to the mainland by a well-populated strip of land, a bare backbone

of mountain stretching through the centre, and fertile valleys edging its shores.
In Lyonesse lived a prosperous and pious
people.   Their churches were a hundred
and forty.   What their farms and gardens were, what must have been the
sweetness of the sandy reaches and the
calm bays, can be imagined by those who
have tasted the airs that are here the
breath of the Gulf Stream, cherisher of
bloom.   But there came a day, says the
story, when doom overtook them; possibly not in haste, — for one man had time
to reach the mainland before, with un-
conquerable might, the sea rose and over-
whelmed his home.   As a matter of
fact, however, it is unknown whether
Lyonesse was slowly eaten away by the
greedy sea or whether it sank under swift
convulsion.   That such a land once existed is upheld by the fact that a neighboring coast region was undoubtedly subject
to the same calamity of tidal overflow;
for of the submerged forests off Mount's
Bay there is historic witness.   Since the
land of Lyonesse lives no longer, save in
imagination, one would fain fancy it to
have been even a fairer and less melancholy spot than Tennyson has made it.

To my own mind, it has a maiden sweetness, a springtime charm, belonging
chiefly to those mystic regions which
"eye hath not seen."

At Glastonbury, ancient nursery of
the British Church, rest the bones of
Arthur and Guinevere. This was the
Isle of Avalon, familiarly known as Avallonia, Island of Apples, from the richness
of its orchards. So let us faithfully believe, even though it is Professor Rhys
who tells us that he feels "warranted
in unmooring the magic spot, and attach-
ing it to the west coast of Cornwall"!

The railway approach to Glastonbury
fills the mind with a new astonishment
at the wonderful diversity of English
scenery. Here the flat monotony of
green field is relieved by hay-ricks and
stacks of black peat. As you near the
town, Glastonbury Tor rises to the south
like a huge cone, surmounted by Saint
Michael's Tower. A ridgy elevation,
extending toward the west, culminates
in Wearyall Hill, natural monument to
Saint Joseph and his blossoming staff.
Scarcely a spot in England has such
store of memories for the antiquarian
and romantic mind. In the year sixty-

three, Joseph of Arimathea and eleven followers, some say sent by Saint Philip of France, landed in Britain, and, led by the Spirit, continued their journey until they reached this ridgy hill. There, weary with wandering, the saint stuck his thorn staff into the ground, and, lo! when he and his companions had rested, they found that the staff had put forth leaf and blossom, — miraculous sign that they should abide in the place. Then did Joseph go down into the valley, and seek the island covered with brushwood, and to-day enriched by the ruins of Glastonbury Abbey, and built a little church of wood, or wattles. There he dwelt and died. A priestly succession kept the place holy; and round about the little wattled church was built one of stone, that the old and sacred walls might be preserved. The present Saint Joseph's Chapel was erected by Henry II.; and the great church at the east of it, connected with it by a galilee, was completed a century after his death. Not only does this spot deserve the reverence due to ancient and consecrated ground, but it is the actual link connecting the Church of the present day with the Christian

worship of ancient Britain. As Freeman
states, it was "the one great institution
which bore up untouched through the
storm of English conquest." On this soil
Saint Patrick dwelt and labored. One
tradition even declares that he was buried
in Saint Joseph's Chapel. Here, too, was
Saint Dunstan's cell, scene of his encoun-
ter with the temptations of a worldly life,
and where he valiantly seized the devil
by the nose. Until Henry VIII.'s van-
dal day, the Abbot of Glastonbury had
almost royal prerogatives in his small but
wealthy domain. He entertained mag-
nificently, often receiving five hundred
guests at a time. To his miniature court
were sent young gentlemen to be fitted
with the accomplishments suited to their
station. The universities were flooded by
his pupils. This, however, was too rich
a field not to attract the scent of the
greedy Tudor, and Henry's commission-
ers settled upon the abbey like a swarm
of locusts. Then good Abbot Whiting
made his fatal mistake : he hid from them
some of the vessels and plate, and, being
discovered, was forthwith accused of rob-
bing his church. Up to the Tower of London was he sent, to be afterwards haled

back, and condemned to death in the hall
of the Bishop's Palace at Wells. But,
with an exquisite refinement of brutality,
he was executed in sight of home, —
drawn on a hurdle to the top of Glastonbury Tor, and there hanged. From this
time of tragic overthrow, the abbey began to fall into decay ; its stones were
used in the town buildings, and even to
pave the roads across the marshes to
Wells. To-day the gray remains, instinct
with a wonderful strength and beauty,
having only lapsed into that desolation
which is never unlovely, sit in the midst
of a green and velvet field.

Saint Joseph's Chapel is still a thing of
wonder, adorned by a wilderness of bush
and weed striving ever to fill its crypt
and smother the foundations. A meagre
but stately portion of the large church
yet remains, rich in two of the magnifi-
cent columns which once separated nave
from choir, crowned now by the wild
rose and pink and yellow sedum. Sheep
are tamely feeding about the enclosure,
and sun and shower bless it, but the
monks, with Arthur and Guinevere, have
been so long fallen into dust that only
their echoing names float back into our

later day. In the reign of Richard I., says tradition, an abbot determined to dig beneath two stone pyramids standing just outside Saint Joseph's Chapel, and evidently placed there as monuments to some important personages. After descending sixteen feet, a coffin was found, hollowed out of an oak-tree. It was in two divisions. One of them, occupying two thirds of the length from the head downwards, contained the body of a man, of such stature that his tibia reached to the middle of a tall man's thigh. In the lower partition lay a female figure, adorned still by one tress of golden hair. At this, however, a monk snatched too eagerly, and it fell into dust. At the same time and place they came upon a leaden cross, bearing the inscription in Latin, "Here lies buried in the Island Avallonia the renowned King Arthur." The bones were afterward removed to the great church, and placed before the high altar, where now the soil into which they have been transmuted nourishes the daisy-starred grass, which is the carpet of ruins. But if the king died not, and was but carried to Avalon for the healing of his wounds, when

shall he return? The story "sometimes
represents Arthur and his men dozing
away, surrounded by their treasures, in
a cave in Snowdon, till the bell of destiny rings the hour for their sallying
forth to victory over the Saxon foe;
sometimes they allow themselves to be
seen of a simple shepherd, whiling away
their time at chess in the cavities of
Cadbury; and sometimes they are described lying beneath the Eildon Hills,
buried in an enchanted sleep, to be
broken at length by one

"'That bids the charmèd sleep of ages fly.
Rolls the long sound through Eildon's caverns vast,
While each dark warrior rouses at the blast,
His horn, his falchion, grasps with mighty hand,
And peals proud Arthur's march from Fairyland.'"

In a field adjoining the abbey grounds,
stands the Abbot's Kitchen, an excellent
example of early domestic architecture.
It is a building square without, octago-
nal within, furnished with huge fire-
places at the corners (wherein one can
stand and look up to the sky), and a
central louvre for light and ventilation.
A cruciform tithe - barn, ancient inns,
and two historic churches also invite
the antiquarian eye. The traveler who

climbs the stony street, lined with
squalid dwellings, to Wearyall Hill will
only be rewarded by a small tablet set
in the ground where stood Joseph's
miraculous thorn ; but all over the town
he will be offered slips from that marvelous tree, which must have been as
wide - spreading as a banyan, to have
been so cut and distributed. However
it came, there is no doubt that Glastonbury possesses a species of thorn —
probably brought from the East — which
blooms twice a year, once at the usual
time and again in the winter, though it
is only by a poetic license which none
but the hypercritical will dispute, that it
is said to open exactly on Christmas
Day.

The ascent of Glastonbury Tor, by an
encircling path, is difficult indeed. On
approaching the breezy summit, one feels
obliged to sit down for frequent intervals of rest, clutching the long grass as
a safeguard against rolling down again.
But once under the shadow of Saint
Michael's Tower, — doubtless a pilgrim
shrine, — such breathless effort is amply
repaid. Below lies Glastonbury, no
longer an island, but surrounded by fair

fields in place of its once glassy streams, and dotted with greenery. Wells Cathedral marks out that little town, like a carven finger-post ; and in the far distance, beyond the Mendips, a shadowy cloud on the horizon, lie the hills of Wales. On the day of my visit two little maids sat together under a sheltering wall, in a field at the foot of the Tor, each with her knitting.

"Is it a very hard hill to climb?" asked I.

"Oh, no, miss," said one, lifting her serious blue eyes for an instant from her work, "it is easy, *quite* easy."

But I did not find it so ; and neither, I fancy, did poor Abbot Whiting, even though he had a hurdle, and had left responsibility forever behind.

THE traveler who would know England in all her moods must assuredly
visit Yorkshire as well as the smiling
Midland counties; and if he be a literary
pilgrim, and would fain understand in
some measure those three great and
lonely spirits, the Brontë sisters, let him
seek out the moors where they walked
and meditated, and vainly explore the region round for one glimpse of the softer
brightness that is the welcome of the
south.

Keighley, on the direct road from
Leeds and four miles from Haworth, has
a comfortable inn, the Devonshire Arms,
where the tourist is made hospitably welcome. It fronts on one of the principal
streets; and seated at its window, the
visitor is within arm's length of crowds
of sickly mill-operatives, standing about
on the pavement during the noon hour,
no doubt discussing the problem of keep-
ing body and soul together, or hurrying
past to the cheerless monotony of their

unsmiling day. Keighley is a frowning town. Its houses are of a dark and dismal gray stone, and the very atmosphere is overspread by that grim and unmistakable look which is testimony that beauty is naught, and use alone has been deified. The most forcible impression made on the new-comer is that the swarming herd of workmen and women are victims of consumption in various stages. A chorus of coughing continually frets the air. You may distinguish all the varied notes of that tragic scale, from the nervous hack of incipient disease to the convulsion destined to shake and tear the body like a destroying fiend. And the faces! young and old, they are pallid, and set in the dogged lines of endurance worn by those who have abandoned all hope, even of earning the daily loaf, should the much-blasphemed will of God afflict them by a dispensation of illness. This was always the cheerful atmosphere of the town nearest Charlotte Brontë's home; and from such grim shelter she went up to London, on a rainy afternoon, to confess the peccadillo of having written one of the greatest novels of her time.

Few influences are more potent than "atmosphere" in determining the bent of sensitive souls. Charlotte Brontë was a creature so fine as to have been affected by every mental and spiritual breath. The most honest and honorable of women, she yet hesitated, at times, in speaking her opinion, because she had not the personal strength needful for sustaining an argument. Her tacit yielding, however, meant only that she could not hold the ground of dogmatic assertion. That all the unseen, intangible influences of life — those airy spirits of the imagined world — affected her most keenly is evident from the self-betrayal in her books, and every jot of evidence from those who knew her best.

"Something seemed near me," she once said, in reference to some moment of prescience, when the invisible proclaimed itself the only real. Hers was not a soul for fear, but one swept and thrilled by every breath of nature or finger of event. What must she have felt when, within the gloomy parsonage walls, she and the two sharers of her vigil expected to hear that pistol-shot which would tell them that Branwell, insane

from opium and misery, had killed his
father or himself? Or when, Anne and
Emily no longer alive, she paced the silent house at midnight, unable to sleep,
her nerves tense with anguish and the
desire to touch some comfort outside
the barren present? Certainly it is most
true that, to judge her character from
the inside, one must actually stand in
the paths where she walked, and scan
her heaven with a studious eye.

It was on a day woven of fanciful fabric, shot athwart with sun, and darkened
by sudden misty showers, that we took
the train for Haworth, and leaving the
station, climbed that steep and stony
street which leads to church and parsonage. There is very little satisfaction in
visiting the church and examining its
shining tablets to the Brontë family, for
the edifice has been rebuilt, and only the
old square tower is an actual memento
of the past. The parsonage, too, has
been remodeled; and though parts of
the kitchen walls have been retained, the
most curious visitor would scarcely find
himself repaid for invading them. But
the churchyard, bleak and populous, is
the same; and there also is that bad

neighbor, the Black Bull Inn, where
Branwell caroused. Still do the "pur-
ple-black" moors, the one delight of
Yorkshire, wear the face with which
they enchained Emily's loyal heart, and
spoke peace to all three battling spirits.

"My sister Emily loved the moors,"
said Charlotte. "Flowers brighter than
the rose bloomed in the blackest of the
heath for her; out of a sullen hollow in
a livid hillside her mind could make an
Eden."

August, or the first of September, is
the gala time for the heather; then is it
in full glory of rose-purple, and prodigal
in bloom. A path leads by the parsonage and through a gate out upon this
free moorland wilderness, where, on a
day of sun overhead and bloom under
foot, one finds a delight and exhilaration
suited to the mountain-tops of life. One
lonely figure only did we overtake on the
afternoon of our visit, — a tall, gaunt
woman, with shawl thrown over her
head, who, swinging her great house-key,
had been to the churchyard where lay
her husband's grave. This was the way
to the "mō-ōrs," she told us, with an in-
describable broadening of the vowels.

This path was called the Brontë Walk,
for Charlotte and her sisters had been
said to delight in it. It was a lonely
region, she confessed. She herself had
come here from the north to be near her
husband's people ; and now he was dead,
and she alone. A forlorn place, — but
the "mō-ōrs" were company. It was
easy to see that they might be, in that
region of gray villages, of sky too often
clouded, of sweeping winds and drizzling
rain. It rained as we walked along the
ling-bordered path, and talked of those
three women whose hearts and lips had
been touched with the immortal fire of
the ideal, and yet to whom duty was ever
that "stern law-giver" from whose decree they could never swerve. As we
wound about one knoll after another of
the curving moor, lo ! the clouds were
swept aside, and blue sky briefly smiled.
What tongue can speak the sad beauty
of the heather with the sun upon it, and
fleeting shadows chasing the light over
low-lying valleys in the distance ! That
day the ling was in full bloom, and
heather, somewhat earlier in its coming,
still showed rosy in the sun-patches.
Ling is far more sober in its general

effect than the common heath ; its tones
are colder, verging on lilac and gray.
Yet, close to the eye, it declares even a
finer grace, a more delicate loveliness,
than those of its hardy sister.   It is the
Quaker maiden of the barren hills.   On
the left, the moor goes billowing on like
the fixed heavings of an amethystine sea.
Leave the path, and take footing in the
crisp heather that crackles under foot
with a husky protest, — a ringing of
whispering chimes, — with the delusive
hope of hurrying to the top of some
knoll forming the horizon line, and from
which you fancy yourself able to see all
the countries of the earth.   It is no easy
task.   Traverse hill and hollow, and
there are still more knolls, heather-cov-
ered, and a new horizon line.   Perhaps
he is happier who does not seek the
highest vantage-ground to over-sweep
villages in distant valleys, but goes away
rich in the certainty that he has not seen
the confines of the moors, and that their
extent is infinite.   On and on sweeps the
heavenly monotony of these brown-gray
solitudes.   If you cling only to the path,
you meet an occasional flock of feeding
sheep ; a tiny watercourse bars the way,

or a dismal stone house, more cheerless
company than none, sits frowning at the
sky.

But what must they be, these bleak
hillsides, when the winter wind rages
across them, and lays waste the land
with his invisible sword ? One shudders
as fancy pictures the spot, and shudders
again, remembering how winter as well
as summer found three tender women
here imprisoned in a hermitage they
loved. Skies might be scowling, and the
heather a withered waste ; indoors they
must sit beneath the shadow of their
father's rigorous life and their brother's
ruin. Yet were they undaunted, and
clung to patience, fanning the fire of imagination until their chilled hearts were
warmer from the glow. Nay, happier
than that, they were still starved and
cold ; but for us, for whom they uncon-
sciously lived, they builded a great bon-
fire ; for they have stirred us anew with
that mighty lesson of the power of the
spirit. O marvelous sway of the few
endowed with the gift we call genius,
that though the body faint, and personal happiness dies or is still-born, they
have yet the strength to build for them-

selves monuments more enduring than
brass, which are as finger-posts to all
other striving souls!

Over a little stationer's shop in the
village was then a sparse collection of
Brontë relics : pencil drawings, finished
with the exquisite care characterizing
every work from Charlotte's fingers, her
little old-fashioned shawl (somehow so
like her that it is more precious than
the whole collection), and various household articles bought from the auction-
sale after her death. The keeper of this
little store of curiosities was a relative
of that Martha who had been Tabby's
helpmate in the kitchen, when she became too old for work, and yet could
not be discharged; and it was through
Martha that many of the articles were
obtained. Now there is a Brontë Soci-
ety and a Museum : strange antitheses
to the seclusion of those shrinking lives.

It is impossible to look at the Black
Bull without an unjust feeling of rancor,
remembering its fascination for Branwell, and its share in his wrong-doing.
It is a small tavern of the gray stone so
unfortunately common in the region, and
such near neighbor is it to the church-

yard that one can easily fancy him leap-
ing from its window into the yard, as he
was said to do, when he heard Charlotte's voice, on her way to seek and
draw him home.

"Do you want some one to help you
with your bottle, sir?" a stranger would
be asked at the inn. "If you do, I'll
send up for Patrick." And then poor
Branwell (or Patrick, as he was familiarly
called) would be swept into those orgies,
of which the very suspicion covered his
sisters with shame and horror.

The actually "passionate pilgrim"
who leaves unturned no stone beneath
which lies the weed of remembrance,
will devote a thought to the Brontës in
London, and walk through Paternoster
Row with the recollection that here
stood the Chapter Coffee-house where
Charlotte and Anne, doubtless through
a long course of years its only women
visitors, spent the few days of their stay
in London. The house was of old and
great renown. Under its roof starving
Chatterton wrote his mother, in that
burst of deceptive pride, "I am quite
familiar at the Chapter Coffee-house,
and know all the geniuses there." It

was once the meeting-place of wit and
scholar; and later, when its fame had
somewhat declined, country clergymen
and university men occasionally sought
it out, to hear what might have happened in the world of letters. The
Brontës, who knew of it through their
father's rare visits, had no idea that they
were doing anything unusual in making
it their stopping place; and it proved a
hospitable and kindly shelter. Think of
the two little creatures clinging together
in a window-seat of the dingy room,
when their publisher came to take them
to the opera, and of their bewilderment
at the noise of "the City" surging
without! Yet Charlotte always declared
she loved the busy City better than the
West End: the one existed for work,
the other for luxury and fashion.

Is there not heavenly significance in
the chord which thrills and tightens
when we approach the dwelling-places of
great and beloved souls, so that we are
drawn to walk in the paths their feet
have trod and look into the skies that
sheltered them? It is more than curi-
osity, more than the satisfaction of a
romantic hero-worship. Do we follow

their earthly footprints with such minuteness because we would "pluck out the heart of their mystery," and learn, if such a thing might be, the secret of that which made them thus? Such influences fostered them, we say, such soil gave them birth. Shall we not be a little nearer — not only them, but the great Source of greatness — if we learn the story of their sojourn here?

It is wisely resolved, and he does well who throws himself into such sympathetic understanding; yet even for him "the greatest is behind." By diligent searching, he shall never analyze the divine spark illuminating the soul with its own radiance of beauty. He can only trace the glow left by its progress, and stop where scientist and Christian alike must pause, at the one unspeakable Name.

143

ONE day at the beginning of our century, Washington Irving, then browsing on the Parnassus grass of England, bethought him of paying a visit to Eastcheap, that home of princely jest and Falstaffian revelry; and he afterwards set down, in delectably humorous English, the story of his attendant search for the old Boar's Head Tavern. The history of that famous inn exists in little, and may be told while the hourglass runs a measure of sand such as Queen Mab might hold upon her palm. When it was built no chronicle relates, but of a certainty it was burned in the Great Fire of 1666. Its successor of the same name, sought out by Goldsmith, who dreamed there of Mrs. Quickly, in the naïve and delightful belief that he was sitting beneath the original roof-tree, had also gone the way of the dead-and-alive who creep too far into a new century. Unfortunately, the old Boar stood in the pathway of progress, and his tenement was first absorbed by shops, and then swept away altogether in 1831, to make way for the approaches to New London Bridge. Now, the site of his former glory is indicated in one meagre line from Baedeker, which incidentally informs the expectant tourist that he will find the monument erected to King William IV. "at the point where King William Street, Gracechurch Street, Eastcheap, and Cannon Street converge; on a site once occupied by Falstaff's Boar's Head Tavern." To be thus minimized, thus dragged in under the shadow of a mere inheritor of crowns, — is it not enough to make fat Jack flash out a lightning - sharp gibe from his limbo, and send some colossal eulogy of self hurtling back into our empty day?

Goldsmith's vision in the tavern rebuilt after the fire deserves remembrance as one of those performances wherein the greatness of the *dramatis personæ* does away with the necessity for correct scene-setting.

"Here," he says, "by a pleasant fire, in the very room where old Sir John Falstaff cracked his jokes, in the very chair which was sometimes honored by

Prince Henry, and sometimes polluted by his immortal merry companions, I sat and ruminated on the follies of youth, wished to be young again, but was resolved to make the best of life whilst it lasted, and now and then compared past and present times together. . . . The watchman had gone twelve. My companions had all stolen off, and none now remained with me but the landlord. From him I could have wished to know the history of a tavern that had such a long succession of customers. I could not help thinking that an account of this kind would be a pleasing contrast of the manners of different ages. But my landlord could give me no information. He continued to doze and sot, and tell a tedious story, as most other landlords usually do, and though he said nothing, yet was not silent. One good joke followed another good joke, and the best joke of all was generally begun towards the end of a bottle. I found at last, however, his wine and his conversation operate by degrees. He insensibly began to alter his appearance. His cravat seemed quilted into a ruff, and his breeches swelled out into a farthingale.

I now fancied him changing sexes; and
as my eyes began to close in slumber, I
imagined my fat landlord actually converted into as fat a landlady. However,
sleep made but few changes in my situa-
tion. The tavern, the apartment, and
the table continued as before. Nothing
suffered mutation but my host, who was
fairly altered into a gentlewoman whom
I knew to be Dame Quickly, mistress of
this tavern in the days of Sir John; and
the liquor we were drinking seemed converted into sack and sugar.

"'My dear Mrs. Quickly,' cried I (for
I knew her perfectly well at first sight),
'I am heartily glad to see you. How
have you left Falstaff, Pistol, and the
rest of our friends below stairs? — brave
and hearty, I hope?'"

There was little left for Irving, the
pioneer of England - loving Americans,
but an hour of musing over past mirth,
and a fruitful gossip (O that some crafty
and unscrupulous listener could have
written us down its story!) with a worthy
woman, self-constituted historian of the
region, and like Mrs. Quickly in being
"a poor widow of Eastcheap." She it
was who suggested that, although he had

necessarily failed in looking upon the
tavern, he might find a picture of it at
Saint Michael's Church, Crooked Lane.
Now, not only had the back window of
the inn looked out upon Saint Michael's
churchyard, but the inn itself had passed
into the hands of the church; the reve-
nues of Bacchus thus reverting to the
Establishment. Nothing therefore could
be more natural than that Saint Michael's
should preserve the counterfeit presentment of its useful ward. But, though
Irving betook himself there without
delay, no such relic was forthcoming.
Countless were the tombs of fishmon-
gers therein, for Saint Michael's lived
near neighbor to Billingsgate. There
also were treasured the ashes of William
Walworth, the doughty knight, most in-
trepid of lord mayors, who smote Wat
Tyler at Smithfield. In the little graveyard adjoining the church stood the
tombstone of honest Robert Preston,
drawer of renown, doubtless the successor of that Francis who had the immortal honor of serving Prince Hal and
Falstaff, — cold comfort all, when the
prime jewel of Eastcheap was lacking.
The sexton, however, perceiving Irving's

disappointment, and reverencing, as English sextons will, the spirit of the loving antiquary, proposed a descent upon the Mason's Arms, at No. 12 Miles Lane. This was the tavern where Saint Michael's vestry held its meetings, as it once had held them at the Boar's Head, departed. Here, too, were deposited its vessels, formerly guarded by the trusty Boar. What he saw there, let Irving himself relate : —

"The old sexton had taken the landlady aside, and, with an air of profound importance, imparted to her my errand. Dame Honeyball was a likely, plump, bustling little woman, and no bad substitute for that paragon of hostesses, Dame Quickly. She seemed delighted with an opportunity to oblige ; and, hurrying upstairs to the archives of her house, where the precious vessels of the parish club were deposited, she returned, smiling and courtesying, with them in her hands.

"The first she presented me was a japanned iron tobacco-box of gigantic size, out of which, I was told, the vestry had smoked at their stated meetings since time immemorial ; and which was

never suffered to be profaned by vulgar
hands, or used on common occasions.
I received it with becoming reverence;
but what was my delight at beholding
on its cover the identical painting of
which I was in quest! There was displayed the outside of the Boar's Head
Tavern, and before the door was to be
seen the whole convivial group, at table,
in full revel; pictured with that wonderful fidelity and force with which the
portraits of renowned generals and com-
modores are illustrated on tobacco-boxes
for the benefit of posterity. Lest, however, there should be any mistake, the
cunning limner had warily inscribed the
names of Prince Hal and Falstaff on
the bottoms of their chairs.

"On the inside of the cover was an
inscription, nearly obliterated, recording
that this box was the gift of Sir Richard
Gore, for the use of the vestry meetings
at the Boar's Head Tavern, and that it
was 'repaired and beautified by his successor, Mr. John Packard, 1767.' Such
is a faithful description of this august and
venerable relic, and I question whether
the learned Scriblerus contemplated his
Roman shield, or the Knights of the

Round Table the long-sought Sangreal, with more exultation.

"While I was meditating on it with enraptured gaze, Dame Honeyball, who was highly gratified by the interest it excited, put in my hands a drinking-cup, or goblet, which also belonged to the vestry, and was descended from the old Boar's Head. It bore the inscription of having been the gift of Francis Wythers, knight, and was held, she told me, in exceeding great value, being considered very 'antyke.'

"The great importance attached to this memento of ancient revelry by modern church-wardens at first puzzled me; but there is nothing sharpens the apprehension so much as antiquarian research, for I immediately perceived that this could be no other than the identical 'parcel-gilt goblet' on which Falstaff made his loving but faithless vow to Dame Quickly, and which would, of course, be treasured up with care among the regalia of her domains, as a testimony of that solemn contract."

There the search rested, so far as Irving was concerned, and he genially remarks, at the close of his paper, that he leaves all this as a rich mine to be worked out by future commentators. " Nor do I despair," he adds, " of seeing the tobacco-box and the 'parcel-gilt goblet' which I have thus brought to light, the subject of future engravings, and almost as fruitful of voluminous dissertations and disputes as the shield of Achilles or the far-famed Portland Vase."

The story of his pilgrimage has, in the mind imbued with romance, a peculiar charm. For my own part, I have never for an instant doubted that the goblet which he identified, with the precision of genius, was actually Mrs. Quickly's, and that goblet I had long resolved to seek, should fortune take me to England.

" Came a day " (speaking elliptically after the fashion of Aurora Leigh), when, on the top of an omnibus, with a faithful gossip, I crossed the Styx of Holborn and Cheapside to that land still peopled by illustrious ghosts, still decked in brave raiment of names that dazzle the eye and stir the blood. Though ancient landmarks have been effaced by hurrying feet, intent on that meat which is less than life, Eastcheap is to-day en-

chanted ground, and its tavern a Mecca
of the mind. The very names in the
neighborhood are redolent of good cheer.
Bread Street, Fish Street Hill, and Pudding Lane each stands pointing a sad
finger to the merry past when, as Lydgate the rhyming monk relates, it was a
city of cooks' shops. Lydgate's period
was that of Henrys IV. and V., and his
London Lackpenny has the ring of good
and olden cheer.

> "Then I hyed me into Est-Chepe;
> One cryes rybbs of befe, and many a pye;
> Pewter pottes they clattered on a heape;
> There was harpe, pype and mynstrelsye."

High revelry was held in Eastcheap in
the time of Henry IV., but, according to
Stow, that most delightful of antiquaries,
who in the face of manifold discourage-
ments added riches untold to the treas-
ury of English history, no taverns then
existed. No man interfered with another's specialty. "The Cooks dressed
Meat and sold no Wine; and the Tav-
erner sold Wine and dressed no Meat
for Sale."

"This Eastcheap," continues he, "is
now a Flesh-Market of Butchers, there
dwelling on both sides of the Street; it

had sometime also Cooks mixed amongst the Butchers, and such other as sold Victuals ready dressed of all sorts. For of old time, when Friends did meet, and were disposed to be merry, they went not to dine and sup in Taverns (for they dressed not Meats to be sold), but to the Cooks, where they called for Meat what they liked, which they always found ready dressed, and at a reasonable rate."

Eastcheap in fact was very near the river, that great highway of London, upon which fish, flesh, and wine were brought to the bank's side. Of that strip of land immediately south, and between Eastcheap and the river, a twelfth-century folio has suggestive mention, thus quoted by Stow :—

"In London, upon the River side, between the Wine in Ships, and the Wine to be sold in Taverns, is a common Cookery or Cooks Row; where daily, for the Season of the Year, Men might have Meat, roast, sod, or fryed ; Fish, Flesh, Fowls, fit for Rich and Poor.

"If any come suddenly to any Citizen from afar, weary, and not willing to tarry till the Meat be bought and dressed ; while the Servant bringeth Water for his Master's Hands, and fetcheth Bread, he shall have immediately (from the River side) all Viands whatsoever he desireth. What Multitude soever, either of Soldiers or Strangers, do come to the City; whatsoever Hour, Day or Night, according to their Pleasures, may refresh themselves. And they which delight in Delicateness, may be satisfied with as delicate Dishes there, as may be found elsewhere. And this Cooks Row is very necessary to the City: And according to Plato and Gorgias, Next to Physick, is the Office of Cooks, as Part of a City."

It was in Eastcheap, moreover, that Prince Hal's two brothers fell out with the watch, an episode which may have served as the germ in Shakespeare's brain whence blossomed such a robust tree of mirth. Near by stood Prince Hal's own mansion of Cold Harbour, the cellars enriched with his father's gift, "twenty casks and one pipe of red wine of Gascoigne, free of duty." What other part of London could Falstaff possibly have chosen for his haunts? Even in the old play of Henry Fifth which preceded Shakespeare's, the Prince declares, "You know the old tavern in Eastcheap!

there is good wine." Thus is this rois-
tering region so famous in contemporary
eulogy that it needs no bush of modern
criticism.

The lover of Shakespeare and of his
Falstaff is conscious of an excited delight in threading these murky streets
of "the City," — worshipful, almost, of
the very ground whereon he treads. He
will stand lost in dreaming while traffic
surges past, and smells are ancient and
fishlike, mindful of memory alone. If,
happily, the ideal is more real to him
than solid earth, he will sweep aside the
orderly rubbish of a modern day, and
by force of fancy reconstruct that house
where "hours were cups of sack, and
minutes capons." Let Falstaff rise, tavern reckoning in pocket, and counterfeit
a moment's life, as "gunpowder Percy"
should have done to fright him. Then
shall we see, entering beneath the tavern's tuskèd sign, "a goodly portly man,
'faith, and a corpulent; of a cheerful
look, a pleasing eye, and a most noble
carriage." Here stood the chair which
made his state, when he dared person-
ate his sovereign; this cushion was his
crown, and here behind the arras did he

snore. Here was discussed that merry
jest at Gadshill, and this is the room
where, in the telling, Falstaff's adver-
saries were so marvelously multiplied.
Here must he have heard the chimes at
midnight, and here was his heart struck
cold with pathetic reminder of his end.
Remembrance throngs upon us, until we
are fain to cry :—

"Banish plump Jack and banish all the world!"

Last and most lustrous memory of all,
William Shakespeare, who saw the house
almost daily, on his way to Blackfriars
playhouse, must often have sought its
hospitable door for his cup of sack and
his merry jest with mine host.

When Lessing confessed that for him
the search after truth was to be pre-
ferred to the goddess herself, he proved
the depth of his true wisdom. Happy is
he who takes a roundabout way to Ely-
sium, and so is pleasantly entertained
upon the road! There is no comparison
for blessedness between his lot and that
of the victim of accurate charts and in-
fallible time-tables. Had Ulysses formed
one of a "personally conducted" expedition, a bankrupt world might well have

bemoaned its loss; for who by searching can find in Cook's circular mention of the Lotophagi, "who for their only nourishment eat flowers," the Cyclops, Nausicaä, or Circe? Yet the Wily One came upon them because he sacrificed not on the altar of accurate and abominable science. If the two Americans who sought Eastcheap one golden day had devoted an hour's study to their problem in the British Museum, they would have wandered less widely in pursuit of their desire; nay, would have concluded that there was nothing left to attain, and thus confined themselves to the region of narrow experience reserved for those who let "'I dare not' wait upon 'I would.'" With the simplicity of ignorance, we expected, though the tavern had been swept away, to lay a finger upon the link forged by Irving with the past; to look upon the Mason's Arms, custodian of box and goblet, and to visit Saint Michael's Church, forever memorable from having held its vestry meetings under the sign of the Boar's Head.

King William's Monument was easily found, and near by lay Crooked Lane, "so called of the crooked windings thereof," though, as we speedily realized, its generous curve had been cut short at the call of traffic. A moment's investigation made it also evident that Saint Michael's Church had in that lamentable doing been swept away. Even after that certainty had settled cold upon the heart, we walked up and down the dingy street, staring beseechingly about, as if perchance, church, tower and all might magically rise. An appeal to policemen and dusty looking idlers who played the rôle of oldest inhabitant bore no consoling fruit. Saint Michael's Church was gone; one and another declared that it had not been there in his day; and when we querulously disputed the wisdom of its removal, we were urged to consider the fair proportions of those newer streets — born to crowd it out of being.

"But be not daunted," at length whispered Hope: "the Mason's Arms may still have such store of compensation as it offered Irving in his quest!"

Therefore we turned our steps in the direction of Miles Lane. There might the heart be warmed by the descendants

of Master Edward Honeyball, Irving's
kindly host, or even Master Honeyball
himself, his century brimmed over and
his race still unfinished. Narrow and
dingy is the way. Bales of goods are
hoisted over the head of the timorous
traveler, who, if he be prudent, takes
to the middle of the street, there to
be jostled by unsavory fish-venders and
bearers of burdens. Such hardships of
progress are of little moment, however,
to one inspired by the hope that he may
presently come upon Dame Honeyball,
hospitably alert in the doorway, over-
coming the scruples of the hesitant traveler, and persuading him that her wine
needs no bush. May he not catch a
glimpse of the serving-maid with trim
ankles, or even a savory whiff of that
mutton which was a-roasting so many
years ago? Vain delusion of the too
alert fancy! The Mason's Arms lives
no longer, save upon Irving's rescuing
page. Covering its former ground
stands a glaringly modern and commonplace "public," whither business men,
boys, and cabbies were that day tend-
ing for a pot of beer, to emerge brush-
ing the foam from appreciative lips.

Yet though that beery seclusion might be reserved for the tippling male, not for such reason would woman, wrapped in the armor of an idea, refrain from penetrating therein.

The traveler in England soon learns that here, as in the economy of nature, nothing is lost, and that axiom will comfort him on many a discouraging quest. Anything which Saint Michael's Church had once possessed must still be church property, and would undoubtedly be kept in this parish, or in a neighboring one. Therefore, in whatever corner of secrecy and darkness its forgotten treasures lay hidden, they might surely be unearthed by the persistent seeker. Such reasonable premises being assumed, what more likely spot could there be for eliciting fact or wildfire gossip than the common meeting-ground of a tavern?

The white-aproned "drawer" would fain have told us all we sought, so said his sympathetic manner, but he could only suggest the beadle as a probable fountain of Eastcheap lore. And where was the beadle to be found? He was in, not five minutes ago, to take his pint of beer, and he might come round again in an hour. (O bibulous beadle, is this thine hourly custom?) It all depended upon what he had to do. Some days there were a good many burials. No beadle, however, was forthcoming, even after long lingering, and an ascent to his room, over three flights of breakneck stairs; and choosing at random a church near by which might divulge hidden information, we went to Saint Margaret Pattens, named for the patten-makers who long ago flourished there, and rich in a store of old-time memories. The white-haired rector was finishing his daily service to empty benches; for, though traffic surges about this and its sister churches in the heart of the City, it is rare indeed that man or woman enters one of them to seek the bread of life. They have their religiously preserved carvings, their precious organs, their careful service; they go quietly beating on, like a jeweled timepiece in the clothes of a beggar, and afar off, but ominous, sounds the howl of "Disestablishment!"

This gentleman was not the rector of Saint Margaret Pattens, protested an inner voice, when finally he was ready to speak with the strangers. He was Trollope's gentle "Warden."

"Have you given up that old and loving habit of fingering your imaginary violoncello?" one refrained with difficulty from asking. "Has Archdeacon Grantly frowned it down, and is he at this moment waiting for you at home. to broach some scheme of advancement in which your cleanly soul will not concur?" The Warden held, as it happily proved, the key to difficulty the first. Saint Michael's parish had, he said at once, been merged in Saint Magnus's, and doubtless took all its property with it. But if we were interested in the Boar's Head, should we not also like to see an entry in Saint Margaret's vestry accounts, of the sixteenth century, proving that it found the tavern a comfortable neighbor? From an old oaken chest he drew a volume, its leather covers worn rough by time, its pages yellowed and stained by years, if not from use.

"*Itn* paide for our dynners on St. Andrewse Day at the Bores Hedde 18*s.* 6*d.*"

He it was who suggested that the parcel-gilt goblet was not a sacramental

cup, but rather one used by the vestry
in its business meetings, which had also
a convivial character. Such cups were
known as "masers," and might be either
of metal or of wood, carved, and orna-
mented with silver and gold. An allu-
sion of the sixteenth century to another
vessel describes it as "a great cuppe,
brode and deepe, such as great masers
were wont to be." These vessels, true
loving-cups, were highly valued by the
fortunate owners, whether individuals or
corporations. The Warden would not
hear of thanks. Old customs were his
delight, he protested, and of all the
phantasms of this changing world they
best rewarded pursuit. He had even
revived in his own church the ancient
ceremony of "beating the bounds." The
children of the parish marched out in
due form and beat with wands the
parish boundaries ; but so changed had
the region become since the days when
such geography lessons were of ordinary occurence, and building had not
smothered God's earth, that one child
had to be let down from a window into
a closed court, to touch with his wand
a separating point. But O times and

manners! that ye have changed is patent in the fact that whereas such occasions served of old as pretext for reveling, to-day but one friendly baker regaled the beaters with buns and lemonade. Where are the cakes and ale whereon they feasted once from door to door? Gone, with bear-baitings, new plays on Bankside, mouth-filling oaths, and good Queen Bess.

With that day and the farewell courtesies of the gentle Warden ended our quest. It even hung fire over the summer, for an appeal by letter to the "fair parish church of Saint Magnus" elicited the fact that it was undergoing repair, and was therefore in no condition for visitors. Thus it happened that it was only a few days before sailing for America that we entered the little vestry, and caught at once from the window a sight more to be desired than the freedom of the city in a box of gold. There, hemmed in by walls, lies a small patch of green, its one ornament the Purbeck stone once in Saint Michael's churchyard to tell the virtues of Robert Preston, and now sojourning with Saint Magnus, still to rehearse his fame.

"Bacchus, to give the toping world surprise,
    Produced one sober son, and here he lies.
    Though reared among full hogsheads, he defy'd
    The charms of wine, and every one beside.
    O reader, if to justice thou'rt inclined,
    Keep honest Preston daily in thy mind.
    He drew good wine, took care to fill his pots,
    Had sundry virtues that excused his faults.
    You that on Bacchus have the like dependence,
    Pray copy Bob in measure and attendance."

Truly, it is good to touch with reverent finger each link of a golden past : to renew our fondness for the motherland by thumbing over the pages of her story ! The rector of Saint Magnus dallied with our impatience, and proffered many a fillip to the appetite before he would produce the nightingales' tongues and ortolans of the feast. We must see his church, redolent of memories ancient and wonderful, and the tablet to Miles Coverdale, wherein the godly and learned do much delight. We must even try his organ. But at length returned to the vestry room, there appeared a sexton, penetrated to the soul with the importance of every detail connected with the Establishment ; and in his hands he bore two boxes, one of wood, and the other the identical tobacco-box of Irving's quest, — the same, yet different in the fresh glory of paint probably applied in 1861, for, as the inscription relates, it was then repaired anew. Now be it understood that there had been throughout little talk of the goblet, but much of this box from which the church-wardens once filled their innocent pipes. It was impossible to refer honestly to the former treasure in any way except as a memento of Mrs. Quickly; and would even the daring scion of an aggressive land approach a reverend incumbent of the English Church with a mention of that amiable but never conventional woman, painful antithesis to the British matron? Perish the thought! Rather wait, hoping that box and goblet had drifted down the stream of years still together, and that the same incoming wave would sweep them to the travelers' feet. With a slow seriousness befitting the occasion the wooden box was opened, and there, in a green baize seclusion, lay the goblet of our dreams. The moment had come, and triumphantly it crowned endeavor. No one who has seen that cup can doubt for a moment that it certainly is the one illuminated by the sea-coal fire that day when Falstaff swore his perishable oath. It is of a goodly shape, with a standard and a generous bowl. It is lined with gold, "parcel-gilt," and the silver exterior is decorated with fanciful little figures in outline, shaped somewhat like Prince Rupert drops. About the foot runs the inscription, *Ex dono Francisci Wythers Armigeri.*

There is an actual possibility connected with this relic which is hardly to be considered without excitement. The cup, we are told, was in the first part of this century "very 'antyke.'" What is more probable than that William Shakespeare, in his social evenings at the tavern where it was kept, was a welcome guest of Saint Michael's vestry, what time the cup went round and beards wagged all? The parcel-gilt goblet was ever held in high esteem, whenever it was first received, and it is easy to believe it formed a part of the church property before 1597, the earliest date to be assigned King Henry IV. That possibility once assumed, the mind runs riot in conjecture, and almost loses its balance in a mad chase after the thistledown of circumstantial proof. Who was

Sir Francis Wythers? When was he christened, married, or where did he die? A list of tombstones and tablets from Saint Michael's contains not his name. Its register of christenings, marriages, and burials, beginning in 1538, holds no reference to him. Did he belong to some other parish, which keeps in hiding the record of his life, waiting for a lucky finder, that prince whose lot it is to succeed after the many fail, or did he go to the wars with Falstaff, to receive burial "unhousel'd, disappointed, unanel'd"?—for it is difficult to avoid a strange mingling of the poetical and real in such a quest. Was he one of the Lancashire Withers, a family adorned by George Wither, the poet, and of whose founder mention is made in the reign of Edward II.? "What's become of Waring?" is no more crucial problem, no blinder scent, than that connected with this elusive donor of a cup. The ingenious mind will suggest that there may be some mention of goblet or giver in Saint Michael's audit books. Even so small a matter as paying for the inscription, if that were not done until after the presentation, would surely

be mentioned. Vain hope! The earliest parochial book is dated 1617, and
has nothing to say on the subject. It
does, however, contain two references
to the Boar's Head, which are of some
interest, like every trifle touching that
wonder-breeding spot.

I, for one, am determined to assume
that the cup has met the eye of Shakespeare, and was even touched by his
good right hand. I shall never allow
the true delight of literary pilgrimage
to be spoiled by too close adherence to
possible fact. In the ideal suppositions
of life lie its paramount charms. He
is a happy man, gifted with the truest
wisdom, who sees in every thorn-tree at
Glastonbury a scion of the olden one,
who can bare his head in memory of
King Arthur at each of the several
places claiming the crown of Camelot,
and people the land with brave men and
fair women who, as the learned tell us,
were never more than "such stuff as
dreams are made on."

Shakespeare dearly loved to harness
every-day events to the car of poesy; to
fit a cart-horse out with wings, and bid
him godspeed in playing Pegasus. When

Titania describes a strange confusion of the seasons, and the resulting evils to man and beast, there can be no doubt that the poet had in mind the year 1594, when "the spring was very unkind, by means of the abundance of rain that fell. Our July hath been like to a February; our June even as an April: so that the air must needs be infected." That immortal speech of Bottom, wherein he entreats the ladies not to tremble, since he is no lion, but "a man as other men are," has its prototype in an incident, probably of Shakespeare's own time, which is recorded in a collection entitled Merry Passages and Jests:—

"There was a spectacle presented to Queen Elizabeth upon the water, and among others Harry Goldingham was to represent Arion upon the Dolphin's backe; but finding his voice to be verye hoarse and unpleasant when he came to perform it, he tears off his disguise, and swears he was none of Arion, not he, but even honest Harry Goldingham."

Face-painting, Mary Queen of Scots and her siren arts, the dancing horse (a justly celebrated wonder of the poet's time), a fool's leap into a custard to excite the popular mirth, the "little eyases" of Saint Paul's Cathedral, who became stage favorites, to be strongly and somewhat jealously censured by legitimate players, — dozens of contemporary allusions illustrate his royal and prodigal way of sweeping up the dust from the path of every-day life and using it for ornament of his pageants.

The "parcel-gilt goblet at the Boar's Head," — a careless mention, fit only to cause a passing smile on such lips as had merrily touched its brim, but to us, cold under the long shadows of too late a day, pregnant with wondrous meaning. For to have looked upon what Shakespeare saw, though it be but the infinitely removed descendants of the daisies that bloomed at Stratford three centuries ago, to have held what his hand once touched, is to have found one vivifying crumb left from that high feast when every man

> "put his whole wit in a jest,
> And resolved to live a fool the rest
> Of his dull life."

THE first significant point of our Warwickshire pilgrimage was Coventry (I refrain with some difficulty from the qualifying "three-spired," since the guide-books have made it all their own), and here an ancient dame, little guessing that graver matters occupied my thoughts, insisted on stopping us in the street, and pointing out the head of Peeping Tom. "Go to, thou 'rt naught!" I could have said, for my mind was busy painting itself a picture of Falstaff's scarecrow army, as it marched hereby to the battlefield where the immortal Jack vicariously slew Hotspur, after fighting that "long hour by Shrewsbury clock." Once begin to imagine that tattered and straggling host, and you will perforce dismiss the Lady Godiva, though with a reverent mind, and consider not architecture, albeit three or thirty spires insistently call : — an army of such as "were never soldiers, but discarded, unjust serving-men, younger

173

sons to younger brothers, revolted tap-
sters, and ostlers tradefallen; the can-
kers of a calm world, and a long peace;
. . . a hundred and fifty tattered prodi-
gals, lately come from swine-keeping,
from eating draff and husks." Moreover, an army which needed not the
outfit of shirts, since, like Autolycus of
blessed memory, it could "find linen
enough on every hedge." But not
always may you stay to hobnob with
fat Jack; a wandering life has many
secondary joys in fee, and presently, in
sober and practical fashion, we engaged
a carriage to take us to the salient
spots of George Eliot's Warwickshire
sojourn. Now for my own part, I do
so heartily agree with her relatives and
friends in their distaste for the prying
tourist who would fain make his way
into their gardens and bedrooms — nay,
into their very linen-chests, in search
of the table-cloths woven by Mrs. Tulliver herself "and bleached so beautiful,"
and marked "so as nobody ever saw
such marking," — that it would take a
strong temptation to draw me into such
forbidden ways. (The temptation came,
in good time, let me whisper, and I

succumbed to it, and was glad!) But it is an ever-growing delight to me to look on the same tract of earth and the very outline of tree and roof which once fed the gaze of heroes. Think of the country about Stratford and its influence on the mind of Master Will Shakespeare, reputed poacher, and lover of Anne Hathaway, — the fruitful earth and ever responsive leafage, the hedges, lavish of bloom, the still-flowing streams, great sky-spaces and far horizon; must they not so have nourished and calmed that great spirit that it could thereafter express itself from a state of serene healthfulness only to be attained in fitful moods by one suffocated in mining damps and glooms, or depressed by the gray wastes of Lincolnshire? And so, in tracing the steps of this woman-genius, it was enough to look at the outside of the Coventry School where she was a shy and earnest student, or at Rosehill, happy scene of her friendship with the Brays, without in the least desiring entrance, and then to drive on to Griff House, where almost a quarter-century of her youth was passed.

During the progress of the road from
Coventry to Nuneaton, Warwickshire
displays a thoughtful and sober face.
The earth is harder and more unyielding than at flowery Stratford. No
longer does it smile unreservedly. Coal
dust has here and there begrimed it;
and at intervals a bare and ugly chimney
points upward a sooty finger in derisive
challenge to the "whip of the skies."
At a glance, one reads here the earth-
doom and history, — the tale of unre-
mitting toil. In sweet farming regions
man may be baptized in his own sweat
and made drunk by his own tears, but
the gracious and deceitful earth only
smiles the more, and makes his home an
outer paradise, so that the thoughtless
onlooker is glad for him, and fancies
the poetic content of days spent in his
picturesque (and mildewed) thatched cottage. But here the harder phases of
living make themselves rudely apparent,
and who can doubt that George Eliot
read from them her first gospel of the
trouble of life?

Now, John, our driver that day, a
most serious man who talked as if he
might have been an intimate acquaint-

ance of the Great Lexicographer, was impressed with a wholesome fear of Mr. Isaac Evans, George Eliot's brother. According to him, this gentleman had suffered much from the settling of tourists upon his roof-tree, very like the plagues of ancient Egypt; and we could imagine that he had threatened our conscientious John with dire vengeance, should he ever bring such harpies that way again. "All hail to thee for a sensible man, O brother of the great!" we ejaculated mentally. "Not for worlds would we invade thy peace!"

"You can walk inside the grounds," said John, drawing up before Griff House. "He won't mind that. But please, miss, don't go into the house!"

Go into the house, like a monster made out of Paul Pry and Peeping Tom! Though American, we were not of that mould, and it was only after repeated urgings from the box that we alighted, and like cats in a cream-rich pantry, took a few cautious steps into the trim door-yard in front of the comfortable brick house. And there temptation laid for our feet its first cobweb snare. A woman, a very decent serving-woman, came walking down the path, and to her we weakly apologized for our presence, adding that we were from over-sea, and that we could not resist looking upon the spot where George Eliot was born.

"She wasn't born here," said this sympathetic and kindly soul, "she was born at Arbury Farm, though she did live here for many years."

This was a blow. We had wasted our emotions, we had wept and applauded in the wrong place, and after a further exchange of civilities we returned to the carriage and taxed John with having made a mistake. (For, to our shame be it confessed, Baedeker had that day been left behind, and memory proved but a yielding staff.) And thereupon he waxed so emphatic, declaring that everybody knew Griff House to be the birthplace of Mary Ann Evans, and moreover, he looked so like a local oracle, destined to develop into an Oldest Inhabitant, that we knew not what to think, and, perplexed and depressed, drove on to Chilvers Coton, the Shepperton of the "Scenes from Clerical Life."

Chilvers Coton, a suburb of dull,

workaday Nuneaton, is not a place to
invite the eye. It is, indeed, "a flat,
ugly district . . . depressing enough to
look at even on the brightest days,"
and the little commonplace church is
close neighbor to a crowded yard of
"the happy dead people." The building
was locked, and thereupon we besieged
the comfortable, old-fashioned vicarage,
to ask for the key. A trim, rosy maid
appeared at the door, and took the
words from our mouths. "The key,
miss? Yes, miss. And perhaps you
wish to see Milly's grave!" So in a
half-dream we entered the little homely
structure, and walked into the very pew
where Mary Ann Evans used to sit, in
those years when, as she confesses,
"my nurse found it necessary to provide
for the reënforcement of my devotional
patience, by smuggling bread and butter
into the sacred edifice." The improve-
ments she once deplored as having
marred the picture retained by her
childish memory have yet left the
church very quaint and characteristic;
the pews are old-fashioned, the gal-
leries delightful. It is easy to feel in
that atmosphere as if one were within

a very few layers of the heart of country life. Then out into the church-yard again, where, surrounded by a high railing and weighted with a heavy tombstone, lies the grave of Emma Gwyther, who died at thirty-four, and whose sad fortunes were mirrored in those of Milly Barton. We left the spot, touched and saddened, as one who has looked on some most sacred relic of the past; wherever Mary Ann Evans was born, we had at least read here one chapter of her thoughtful, image-storing childhood. Thereupon, like a persistent insect, came buzzing back the forgotten question, "Marry, *where* was she born?" Not that it made any difference, since she once walked among us, but that the spirit of investigation forbade inglori-ous defeat. And then it was that a new version of Launcelot Gobbo's im-mortal dialogue between conscience and the fiend was again enacted, and with the world-old result. "Run!" cried the fiend in conclusion, and we said to our driver, "Back to Griff House!" set our lips and abided the event. I think John must have suspected us of contem-plating some deed of darkness, for he was in his turn resolute of countenance, as if, should Mr. Evans charge upon the besiegers, he had made up his mind to fly, hot-foot, to Coventry, leaving us in the lurch. But prudence had been quite abandoned with decorum, and walking up to the teeth of the enemy, we knocked for admittance at the door of Griff House. Then appeared again the decent serving‑woman, and we threw ourselves on her mercy. We were tossed about by winds of doctrine; would she tell us her grounds for saying that Mary Ann Evans was not born here? She smiled, as if it made very little difference, and yet indulgently, as one might over the vagaries of uneasy Americans, inclined to spend their nervous energy in fighting windmills and hunting lions, and repeated her tale. But in the midst of it she stopped to listen, evidently to a call from within, and, after a word of apology, hastened up the stairs. She was soon back again, this time bearing a message. "Miss Evans says you may walk in the garden, miss, if you like." (Poor Miss Evans! should we take this as the spontaneous impulse of a kindly heart, or was it a sop thrown to un-

known barbarians, whom she expected
presently in her bed - chamber?) At
all events, we stayed not to question
motives, but betook ourselves, with our
gentle-mannered guide, to a fascinating
old-fashioned garden at the back of the
house, and there it was that an excit-
ing and terrible event befell. For she
suddenly exclaimed, in an undertone,
"There is Mr. Evans himself! You
can ask him where she was born!" and
fled, leaving us in the presence of a
tall, powerful man, clad in gray, and
pushing a lawn - mower. There was
nothing for us to do but flee also, or
brazenly advance; to our everlasting
discredit, be it recorded that we chose
the latter and ignoble course. Now, I
confess that when I fell into talk with
this quiet English land - agent, it was
from a mood as uplifted and delirious
as that of one who should "see Shelley
plain," for it was borne in upon me that
here, in the flesh, was Tom Tulliver,
honest, stanch, indomitable of will, —
yet not of wide vision and ever conscious of his own infallibility. ("And
the worst of it is," once said a clever
woman, "that he not only thought so,

but according to recognized standards Tom always *was* right.") This was the man with whose being George Eliot's own was knit during the most plastic period of her life, who could admit her to the highest heaven of happiness, as Tom had ever the power of doing in his intercourse with Maggie, and whose disapproval, even over so small a matter as the jam puffs, would poison the very fountain of her content. This was he of whom she wrote,

> "My doll seemed lifeless, and no girlish toy
> Had any reason, when my brother came."

It was Tom, the real or imagined Tom, who praised her because, in a moment of still and happy dreaming, she caught a big fish, and learned thereby how "luck is with glory wed." It was Tom who was separated from her by that awful soul-distance brought about by "the dire years;" who perchance condemned where he could not understand, and drew from her at length the home-sick cry,

> "But were another childhood-world my share,
> I would be born a little sister there."

Here, for all present purposes, was Tom Tulliver, gray-bearded, with keen

yet kindly gray eyes and a slow sad
voice, — and oh, wonder! with George
Eliot's own Dante nose. Do you remember when sweet Mary Seraskier came
back to Peter Ibbetson from the outer,
or mayhap the inner world, how he
tried so vainly, in his waking moments,
to recall her utterances, and put them
into the language of every-day thought
and speech? Thus it happened when I
talked with Tom Tulliver. I meant, for
my own after-delight, to remember his
phrasing exactly as it left his lips, but I
can only repeat it now, hopelessly Amer-
icanized.

"No, she was not born here," he said.
"She was born at Arbury Farm, and
brought here when she was but six
months old."

"And which was her window? Where
is her room?"

"Why, she was everywhere about the
house," he answered, in his ponderous
fashion. "She *lived* here."

But it was evident that the George
Eliot of universal fame was less to him
than the little sister whose "tiny shoe"
he had guided over the stepping-stones,
so many years agone. He was half

touched, half perplexed that we should
be thus moved over the traces of their
vanished youth.

"You came from America?" he asked.
"It's a long way."

And then, when we stammeringly
tried to tell him how we had first of all
sought Shakespeare's home, inevitably
to make this the second step in our
pilgrimage of praise and worship, his
reserve seemed to break up, as if, she
being dead, he would thank the humblest
soul for having loved her.

"And you've been to the church?"
he asked. "Ah, they've altered it!
You may see the pew where she used to
sit, but in those days its walls were so
high that she had to stand up on the
seat to see the singers." (Still dreaming over the child, and not the girl or
woman! Did she know, and was it an
abiding joy that ever, in the home of his
mind, she dwelt "a little sister"?)

Needless to say that we did not linger,
afraid of outstaying his tolerance.

"And you will go to Arbury Farm?"
he asked, adding, after full directions for
finding it, "Tell them I sent you."

We left him in his garden and wan-

dered at will for a moment, casting un-
seeing eyes at the farm buildings and
populous yard, where little Maggie light-
heartedly trudged about, or brooded over
the "bitter sorrows of childhood."

It was all so faithful, so real! and
nothing more so than the true presentment of Tom, grown to man's estate.
This was the apex of human experience, so far as our present quest was
concerned; not only could we imagine
the outer life of the fine spirit forever
vanished, but we had seen him who was
so responsible for a vast part of its
emotional stress. Yet there was, and
is to-day, a bitter drop in that jeweled
cup; we had behaved like the tradi-
tional American whose gospel is "Push,"
and had earned thereby the condemna-
tion pronounced upon such from of old
by the courteous and the gentle. One
grace only was left in us; we kept our
own counsel, lest other intrusive spirits,
possibly worse than the first, should repeat our deed, and still further persecute
our patient host. But time and fate
between them have taken the seal from
our lips, — for the master of Griff House
is dead.

It is the eccentric dower of some to grow quite as hot-headed and tremulous over a prospective needle in a haymow as ever Midas could have been on receiving his gift. To such, Knutsford, in Cheshire, offers a perfect hunting-ground for that sort of plunder so humorously resembling Gratiano's reasons: "You shall seek all day ere you find them; and when you have them, they are not worth the search." No more satisfying occupation can be invented in this ancient world than the pursuit of what does not absolutely exist, if only the hunter be just credulous enough; bold in belief, yet "not too bold." He must cling to his guesswork with a dauntless zeal; at the same time he shall, for his own ease, recognize the probable futility of such doggedness. For to reconstruct a habitation on the base of some foregone romance is to strike a balance between special disappointment and a vague general joy.

The present Knutsford, *in toto*, is emphatically not the Cranford of Mrs. Gaskell's homely chronicle, but it glitters with links of similitude; moreover, a certain quaintness all its own is continually stimulating the mind to comparison between the fancied and the real, as living perfumes summon forth old memories. Here, at least, Mrs. Gaskell was a child, the little Elizabeth Cleghorn Stevenson, storing up fragmentary impressions easily retraced by one who has lived even a full day in the town; here she was married, and in the green and pleasant yard of the old Unitarian Chapel she lies, with her husband, under lilies of the valley and the constant evergreen. The prospect of figuring in biography was never quite to her taste, and the simple facts of her life offer little temptation to literary gossip-mongers. Her mother was a Holland, of the family represented now by Lord Knutsford. Little Elizabeth was born at Chelsea in 1810, and it was after her mother's death that she was sent to live with Mrs. Lumb, a widowed aunt, at Knutsford, where she remained until marriage took her to permanent residence in Manchester. Both her husband and her father were Unitarian clergymen, and one can guess at her own gracious influence among that slowly growing sect, a power as moving as in literature and the practical walks of trade. It is an old story that her fiction taught the rich some of those trenchant lessons known at first-hand only by the poor; but another deed, more golden yet, shall be remembered of her, — the creation of Cranford, a book to be loved so long as there are smiles and tears in this April world. Who could aspire to uncover its living presentment? One might as well hope, some fortunate London hour, to stumble on Queen Bess setting forth in state to bull-baiting or the play.

The region skirting Knutsford on every hand is rich in memories, but, better still, it offers a loving welcome to the eye. It is a placid, smiling country, diversified by great estates and happy in fat farmlands. Great herds of cows idle about, given over to that industry which is no more than a drowsy day-dream; cropping and chewing, and transmuting the riches of the common sod into such milk and cheese as need only naming for praise. Within the circle of this abounding prosperity lies the little town (ford of the great Canute, some say, with reason), a lovable spot, irregular and pleasing, with individual corners and passages covered by the dust of years, and delighting in their burial. It is presided over by two precise and respectable inns, both mentioned "by name" in Cranford. So many of the strings of trade here are held by women that it is still approximately, as in Cranford days, "in possession of the Amazons." No state of things could be more pleasing to us who would have time "stand still withal," and on the strength of it we may undoubtedly assume that, even in our present year of grace, "to be a man" is, in this delectable place, "to be 'vulgar.'"

Our course thither lay through Manchester (Drumble), where we made brief halt to glance at the Unitarian Chapel, the old preaching-ground of the Reverend William Gaskell, and we reached Knutsford on the eve of a festival calculated to rend dear Miss Matty with deeper doubts than such as embittered her first half-hour at Signor Brunoni's exhibition. For the next afternoon had been set apart for May-day celebration, and Knutsford was already the scene of a wild saturnalia. It had lost its head in anticipatory delirium. It was baking and brewing for a probable influx of visitors by excursion train. The very air was tinged with the aroma of hot cakes, and landladies who on any other day would have curtsied profoundly in Shenstonian welcome, actually held their door-stone against us as though we were marauding Scots, or the rogues and vagabonds of a later interdict, explaining: "It's so very, very awkward, miss, but to-morrow I shall be so busy; and I could hardly give you the attention I should wish. I'm very sorry, miss, but you see how it is, miss, I'm sure;" with that ingratiating lift at the end of the sentence so commendable on an English tongue.

And so perforce we went to an inn, choosing, in deference to Cranford prejudice, one under the firm and affable sway of two ladies. At that modest

choice, said we, the Honorable Mrs.
Jamieson would have been the better
pleased. All that evening the delirium
of hope and expectation continued.
Swings had been erected on the large
open space still known as "the Heath."
Red-and-gold gondolas, cannily set upon
springs, were gayly sliding about in
a magic circle, — a lurid Venice. A
strange aerial railway consisted of one
strong wire high in air; little wheels
with handles on either side were
arranged to fit it, and Darby or Joan,
holding to the handles with desperate
grip, went trundling through space like
gibbeted criminals taking to the sky.
The company of psychologists shall
henceforth be augmented by the man
who classifies the soul according to the
bodily contortions induced by an aerial
railway. I know not what he should
be called, but his course of action will
be plain. Especially in the case of
womankind might he pronounce an
unerring judgment, — for some among
the lassies curled their dangling feet
decently beneath their skirts, some let
them fly amain; others swayed like willow wands; but the many swept on their

playful way like very statues. In all there was one strange likeness: they took their pleasure "sadly," as became true Britons. No face relaxed; not a feature gave way to emotion lighter than a rigid determination to reach the goal. With the onlookers, the same seriousness prevailed, so that when the transatlantic observer gave way to hysterics of mirth, she was regarded, not frowningly, but with a solemn compassion which was in itself hopelessly upsetting. And over all the din of decorous joy amid which the Knutsford youth thus disported itself arose the voice of china-venders and toy-merchants, the cry of those who would fain cloy their countrymen with gruesome lollipop and other sweets, made only to be shunned. Miss Debōrah could never have approved! We tried to cloak our delight under a decent thoughtfulness, and went home to bed. I think we should even have read a counter-irritating chapter of Rasselas had that very eminent work been at hand.

Next day, Knutsford dissolved in rain, and the bakeries may well have wept also. No crowd of excursionists to race

into the town like an invading flood,
some ripple of which must surely inun-
date the humblest eating-houses! They
sank beneath their sweets, like Tarpeia
under her bribe, and the cardboard legend of "Tea" at every door fell into
pulp and sadness. We too had hoped
for a sunny May-day; but, being mortal,
we could not refrain from an acrid reflec-
tion that many a landlady must now be
repenting her short-sighted refusal of us.
Last night we were minnows, for there
were other fish in the sea. To-day we
loomed as the leviathan, and we bore ourselves proudly.

Only a few optimistic citizens had
summoned the spirit to sand the sidewalk in front of their houses, an ancient
custom once accompanying Knutsford
weddings, and still employed on days of
high festival. Still, no one exerted his
genius to the utmost; for though the
sand had been applied in patterns, they
were quite simple, suggesting none of
that elaboration and originality of design
in which Knutsford can indulge when
she chooses. But though the rain could
bully her into curbing her handiwork,
it could not dampen her poetic ardor.

Across the street, from one sandless
sidewalk to the other, swept a banner,
and this was the proud legend thereof : —

> "All hail ! All hail thee, Queen of May !
> For this is our universal holiday ! "

A melancholy dryness, flecked by
uncertain gleams of sun, succeeded the
forenoon, and we betook ourselves, with
an unadulterated joy, to the Heath,
where we sat, chilled and happy, on the
grand stand, watching the festival, and
reconstructing the play-day of Old England from the too sophisticated pleasures of the New. This was May-day
decked out in modern fripperies for the
public entertainment, but it was not
impossible to spy, beneath its lendings,
the simpler sports of a long-past time.
The procession was an historical pageant
of high degree. Here walked Sir Walter Raleigh, Lord Nelson, the Duke
of Wellington, Dick Whittington, and
Robin Hood, none of them over four
feet high. Jack-in-the-Green danced,
bear - wise, under an inverted cone of
hemlock ; the morris - dancers (lithe,
bonny youths, dressed in blue velvet
kneebreeches, white shirts, plaid sashes,

and stockings of a vivid pink seldom
seen outside a lozenge jar) wove a simple
rhythm of movement entrancing to the
eye, and the May queen rode in state,
a pygmy lady of fashion, clad in white
satin, elaborate, frosty, like a wedding-
cake. But one would fain have seen
her in simple white muslin enriched
only with posies of her own plucking,
gathered with the dew on them while
even Corinna slept. "Wake and call
me early," that I may hook myself into
a ball dress and send for my wired
bouquet! Some bathos comes with
time.

But of all that winding throng one ob-
ject alone had power to thrill the mind,
—an old sedan chair, borne midway in
the procession. Do you remember it in
the annals of Cranford? Within that
very chair did Miss Matty sit, tremulous
but resolved, after the social evening at
Mrs. Forrester's, when the dear ladies
scared one another into panic with con-
fession of the bogies most to their mind.
From its unsafe seclusion did she cry
aloud when the men "stopped just where
Headingley Causeway branches off from
Darkness Lane: 'Oh! pray go on!

What is the matter? What is the matter? I will give you sixpence more to go on very fast; pray don't stop here.'" Dear relic of a time more real than our to-day! Knutsford holds nothing more precious.

The Maypole dance was given over to a set of decorous little girls in flower-like dresses, green and pink. They tripped it prettily, they braided and wove their ribbons round the pole, but the spontaneous joy of Old and Merrie England was not in them. A dancing-master had trained them for the public eye. Step and look were no longer the springing welcome to a day when lads and lassies should no more be able to hold their fervor than trees their budding strength. To watch these puppets tripping it was to give way for a moment to sadness, reflecting that nowadays we are ashamed to be merry after we have come to man's estate. We give over our great festivals to children, and then sit looking on with a maddening tickle in the bones that ache to join them.

With another day Knutsford had assumed her wonted air of quiescent decorum. It proved easier to see her now

for what she is, a Georgian town imbued
with the spirit of elegance and precision;
easy, too, to find Cranford in her every
look and word. On that morning began
our trial of local intelligence and belief.
But a step from the Angel Hotel (where
Lord Mauleverer very wisely took up his
quarters, though doubtless when it still
remained on the other side of the way)
stands the Royal George, once living
content under its swinging sign of the
saint militant, but now thrown into self-
contradiction by the swelling adjective
assumed after the Princess Victoria and
the Duchess of Kent had spent a night
under its roof. (An affectionate trait in
this loyal people, to weaken a saint's pat-
ronymic by courtly prefix.) Now it was
this same George which was sought out
by Miss Pole on an idle morning, when
nothing more importunate prevented her
from strolling up the staircase, on benev-
olence intent. For, said Miss Pole, "my
Betty has a second-cousin who is cham-
bermaid there, and I thought Betty
would like to hear how she was." And,
quite by chance, she found herself in
the passage leading from the inn to the
Assembly Room, and then in the room

itself, where Signor Brunoni was making his preparations to juggle the wits
out of Cranford the very next night.
This was the room where, on that bewildering evening, the ladies of Cranford
were so astounded by the resources of
magic that they began to debate whether
they had been in the right " to have come
to see such things," and settled down to
an unalloyed enjoyment of the evening
only on learning that the " tall, thin, dry,
rusty rector," insured against feminine
wiles by a cohort of National School
boys, sat "smiling approval." Memory
more endearing still, it was the Assembly Room where Miss Matty sighed a little over her departed youth, and walked
" mincingly, . . . as if there were a number of genteel observers, instead of two
little boys with a stick of toffy between
them with which to beguile the time."
To seek it out was like dreaming over a
bit of dear Miss Matty's shawl or a print
of her turban.

The George is rich in modern antiquities, — carven balustrades, beautiful old
clocks, and precious work in brass. It
is a living example of the actual magnificence which may be wrapped about

an inn when it has maintained itself in
dignity, and conceded nothing to the
flight of time or change of ownership.
Something stately lies in its hospitable
repose. Like the ladies themselves, it
clings resolutely to old possessions,
though all the world without may clamor
for the changes falsely named improve-
ment. Owing to that deplorable lack
of understanding which is incident to
the present of any age, we were conducted, with flourish of pride, through
the George to the new Assembly Room,
aggressively fresh against the background of Cranford legends, and that
night tricked out with masonic regalia.
"Is this *all?*" cried we, in unhappy
duet. "Has the old hall been quite
swept away?" By no means! Did we
wish to see that? "A very plain room,
miss!" And thither were we led, to
find it shabby, ancient, lovable, — its
tinted walls, dull as a fading memory,
reflecting to the seeing eye a hundred
scenes of innocent yet decorous revelry.
Here Miss Matty took her dainty steps
in the *menuets de la cour,* her young
head, crowned with its soft thick locks
("I had very pretty hair, my dear," said

Miss Matilda), sinking in shyness super-
added to decorum when young Holbrook
came to lead her to the dance. Here she
should have worn the muslin from India
that came to her too late, poor Matty.
Here, too, Miss Pole gleaned the fruitful
grain of gossip, to sow it carefully again ;
for in youth as in age Miss Pole must
ever have been the mouthpiece of the
world which tattles and denies. Somehow I can never connect Miss Debōrah with the Assembly Room. I fancy
she was but an abstracted figure at the
balls ; wishing herself away in a more
serious atmosphere, dreaming over the
ponderous delight of sitting at home
and writing the charges of the archdeacon she was so eminently fitted to
marry.

In the old days, the George had gates
of its own, but now a free passage leads
under the building (somewhat in the
fashion of Clovelly's wayward street),
past the stables, and up a slope, where,
directly facing the pedestrian who as-
cends that way, stands a shop, pointed
out by universal acclaim as the one
where, after the downfall of her fortunes, Miss Matty sold tea and scattered

comfits. It is presided over by an excellent chemist, a man of solemn aspect and an unconscious humor. A tradition lurks in Cranford that he was once sought out by the Unitarian clergyman of the town, on the supposition that he was an adherent of that faith. The crucial question was asked.

"Oh, ay," responded master chemist, "I am a Unitarian. Indeed, sir, I'm almost an agnostic!" Rude, belligerent word to have penetrated the sacred pale of Cranford!

We entered the tiny establishment on some ostensible errand.

"Is this Miss Matty's shop?" we inquired incidentally, the while our purchase was sought.

"Yes, miss," was the unhesitating answer. "We are repairing the back room a bit, or you could see the little window she used to peep through when she heard a customer."

Was reality so wedded to fiction? Actual windows and imaginary Miss Mattys were here in droll conjunction. Further questioning elicited a reason strangely alluring from the very emphasis informing the chaos of its terms.

For it seems that there was in town an aged gentlewoman, the only existing link between old times and new, who chanced to enter the shop after the paper had been torn away, disclosing this tiny window ; and she from her stores of memory drew the assertion that this was Miss Matty's window, because she had seen it many a time and recognized it at once. Amorphous logic and fortunate conclusion !

"Now," said we encouragingly to master chemist, "of course you know all the places mentioned in Cranford?"

"Oh yes, miss," was the cheerful reply.

"Where did the Honorable Mrs. Jamieson live?"

He hesitated. He looked at us wildly. "Amen stuck in" his "throat."

"Give me time to think," he rejoined appealingly ; and, being merciful, we gave it.

Yet, returning that afternoon, and the next day also, with the query, "Have you had time to think?" we were always courteously but sadly answered, "No."

But authorities are not far to seek. The Reverend George A. Payne knows

his literary Knutsford as the Reverend
Henry Green knew its historical and
archæological aspect, and his guesses
are both satisfying and clever. He suggests that the Honorable Mrs. Jamieson occupied a prosperous-looking house
near the lower end of the town, where
the old Unitarian Chapel still holds its
place. I am glad to think so. It is a
residence eminently fitting for that social
paragon, and it requires no impossible
stretch of fancy to see Carlo lumbering
about the yard, winking at the ladies
whom he mulcted of cream, or to catch
at least a glimpse of majestic Mr. Mul-
liner reading the Saint James's Chronicle, while the Cranford dames regard
him from without in controlled and im-
potent wrath. Not far away, moreover,
inclosed by high, invulnerable walls, is
Darkness Lane, subject of that ever
memorable controversy on the night of
the panic, when Miss Matty would fain
have had the sedan chair "go on very
fast," and Miss Pole outbid her by sixpence and induced the men to strike
into the less ominous Headingley Causeway.

At the other end of the town, not far

from the gates of Tatton Park, still
sleeps the old vicarage, a modest dwelling in a circling yard, — that yard where
poor Peter played his little comedy destined to end in grief. Who does not
remember it, — how Peter dressed himself in Debōrah's gown and bonnet, and
juggled a pillow into the semblance of
a baby in long clothes, and how the rector came upon him as he paraded himself and his charge before the gaping
townsfolk? The rest of the story is too
sad for any but sunny days; for Peter
was flogged and ran away to sea, as
every one knows, while the rector re-
pented his angry vengeance in the ashes
of old age, and the gentle house-mother
died awaiting her boy's return.

The actual spots connected with Mrs.
Gaskell's life in Cranford need no broidery of fancy. Looking over the Heath
stands the comfortable, dignified house
where she lived with Mrs. Lumb. Hers
was not an altogether untroubled childhood, suggests Mrs. Ritchie, and she
pictures the little girl running "away
from her aunt's house across the
Heath," hiding "herself in one of its
many green hollows, finding comfort in

the silence, and in the company of birds and insects and natural things." At that time, the Heath was less of a trodden village common than to-day, more populous with birds, richer in furze and leaf. But though the identical house has been enlarged and repaired, its character of homelike comfort is unchanged. There are happy windows, with great window-seats, looking out over the Heath and into the garden at the back. Sun and light are everywhere, and in the garden beds lie the richness and beauty of old-fashioned flowers.

But of all spots made to please the memory and stir it with suggestions not to be denied is Sandlebridge Farm, where lived the Hollands who were Mrs. Gaskell's maternal ancestors. An agreeable though unexciting walk leads to it, between fields green with the wonderful grass that goes to the making of Cheshire cheese, and golden with buttercups. Such far reaches of field and valley are here as to make a not unpleasing loneliness in the land, even under full sunlight ; and when, approaching the farm, you come to a smithy and

mill dedicated to the uses of life, still
the illusion is not dispelled. For in the
smithy two or three leisurely men lean
and look in the intervals of smiling talk,
and the mill, sweet and dusty from the
breath of grain, goes on working quite
by itself. Great wooden beams, heavy
wheels, and dusty hoppers seemed, that
day, to be living a life of uncompanioned
yet happy activity, and from without
came the *plash, plash* of willing water
and the trickle of the feeding stream.
In the hazy distance loomed Alderley
Edge, a mammoth ridge rising above
the hidden caverns where nine hundred
and ninety - nine horses stand "ever
caparisoned and ready for war."

Mrs. Gaskell, when a little girl, must
often have visited the farm to play with
the Holland children; but the spot has
another distinction, more potent still;
for Sandlebridge is Cranford's Woodley,
where Mr. Thomas Holbrook lived, and
read "my Lord Byrron," and ate his
peas happily without the aid of a fork,
and where Miss Matty came to him too
late. The great stone balls are gone
from the pillars beside the gate (the
great Lord Clive used to jump from one

to the other, when he was a schoolboy
at Knutsford), and the ancient decorum of the manor has subsided into the
well-being of a prosperous farm ; but the
spot is full of a slumberous peace. We
were entertained in the stone - flagged
kitchen, with its dresser of blue dishes
on the wall and its flitches of bacon
hanging from the hooks above, and we
drank our milk and ate the sweet farm
bread with a drowsy sense that somehow dear Miss Matty was with us, and
perhaps the sonsy Mary who tells the
tale. Do you remember how Mary
walked about the garden with that an-
tique lover who loved no more, listen-
ing to his comments on flower and leaf ;
and how she afterwards went with him
to the fields, where he forgot her and
strode on to the measure of his dearest
rhymes ? No beauty of the growing
world had lain afar from his full and
lonely life. With us, too, did he walk
that day. The sweet - smelling plants
were such as his eye must have cherished ; the cropping cattle over the
happy slopes were of one family with
those he had fostered ; and the trees,
black-branched and glossy in their green-

ness, had made the tutelary deities of
his land. It is not easy to tell how
peacefully these fields and meadows
slept under the warm sky, nor how lavishly they promised response to loving
tillage.

Slight hints, garrulous suggestions,
are constantly appealing to one in Knutsford, not as literal duplicates of Cranford
customs, but as links in an affectionate
chain of inference. Fiction is not portraiture, but it may easily become a
record of those fleeting impressions
which make an intrinsic part of the
mental tissue. Names familiar to a
writer's youth have a way of creeping
into her work, — nooks and corners,
remarkable for no story of their own,
crop up again when her dreams demand
actual habitat. In reading the history
of Cheshire, it is curious to note the
number of Peters of eminent memory,
and more curious still to stumble on the
name in the yard of Knutsford parish
church. It was not only of good repute,
but very commonly used. Cranford, too,
has adopted it; for did not the local
grandee of Turveydropsical memory figure as Sir Peter Arley, and was not

the rector's erring Peter named for him ?
And let it be said incidentally that no
one who visits that churchyard should
omit reading the epitaph of the Reverend John Swinton, of Nether Knutsford;
for it must assuredly have been written
by Miss Debōrah herself, under direct
inspiration from the ever admirable Doc-
tor Johnson.   Thus it runs:—

" He was happy in an excellent natural Genius, improv'd with every Branch
of polite and useful Learning. His Com-
positions were correct, elegant, nervous,
edifying, and deliver'd with peculiar
Force and Dignity. His Conversation
was courteous, entertaining, instructive,
and animated with a striking Vivacity of
Spirit. As a Husband a Friend and a
Neighbor He was affectionate, faithful,
benevolent, A zealous Assertor and an
able Defender of religious and civil liberty. With Talents which would have
adorn'd the highest Station in the
Church For reasons to himself unan-
swerable He declin'd repeated Offers of
Preferment from his Friends many Years
before his Death.   He bore his last
Affliction with a Firmness and Forti-
tude truly Christian and died lamented

by the Wise, the Learned and the Good Dec. 10th 1764, in the 70th Year of his Age."

Surely six-footed eulogy can no further go!

Another suggestion of Cranford lies in the fact that an actual Arley Hall exists to this day, the seat of the Warburtons, within easy driving distance of Knutsford. Mrs. Gaskell aimed at no needless portraiture or exact topography; but names doubtless got into her mind, and lived there, like an old song, till memory shook them forth. The Cranford scare, moreover, when an hysteria of panic prevailed, and blew prudence out of the ladies' heads while it coaxed some goblin in, — what was that but a refluent wave of Mrs. Gaskell's possible shrinking when, a child, she heard the common reminiscences of the highwayman Higgins? This was the Duval of Knutsford, who lived at the Cann House on the Heathside (neighbor to Mrs. Lumb), and who made nothing of flying over the roads to commit a murder at Bristol and returning again, within forty-eight hours, to prove his alibi. It was Higgins who, living the jolly life of a prosperous gen-

tleman, one night left the ball (held, no
doubt, in the old Assembly Room) to lie
in wait for Lady Warburton and reap
her jewels. But the lady's keen sight
and innocence of mind proved her salvation; for, putting her head out of the
carriage as the robber approached, she
called serenely, "Good-night, Mr. Higgins! Why did you leave the ball so
early?" And Higgins, thus thrust back
into his rôle of country gentleman, rode
on discomfited. He was executed at
Caermarthen in 1767, only forty-three
years before Mrs. Gaskell was born.
This was not too long a period for tradition to linger, painting him ever more
gloomily, until he loomed large, like Guy
of Warwick or Thor the Thunderer.
What affrighting falsities might have
garlanded his name in Knutsford similar
legends all the world over may attest.
Did the sensitive little child, playing
in corners, overhear the Cranford ladies
relating his bold, bad deeds, and trick-
ing them out with bewildering details of
their own device? Did the child herself tremble at the spectre of Darkness
Lane huddling under the mantle of a
pitchy night? Such emotions are the

willow twigs of memory; swept down a living stream, they are bound to reach roothold, and there bud greenly in the vesture of the vernal year.

One curiously suggestive incident belongs to Mrs. Gaskell's own life, though to dwell on it too definitely might serve merely to establish a false bond between the concrete and the ideal. Her only brother, a lieutenant in the merchant service, disappeared on his third or fourth voyage, about the year 1827, and "never was heard of more." Might such lingering tragedy have been the secret of her pathos over the heartbreak and sickness born of Peter's absence? Did she know by too near experience what it is to listen for the footstep that never falls? But one last proof clinches the argument that Knutsford is Cranford, though "some volke miscalle it." Turn to the annals of Cranford, and you shall read of a certain old lady who had "an Alderney cow, which she looked upon as a daughter." Now, this cherished animal, falling into a lime pit, was denuded of all her hair, and her adoptive mother, being ironically recommended to "get her a flannel waistcoat and flannel drawers," did indeed send her thenceforth to pasture soberly clad in gray.

Return now to the chronicles of concrete Knutsford, and listen to the Reverend Henry Green, who, in spite of this one concession, never believed in any intentional literary apotheosis of his cherished town : —

"A woman of advanced age, who was confined to her house through illness, . . . asked me to lend her an amusing or cheerful book. I lent her Cranford, without telling her to what it was supposed to relate. She read the tale of Life in a Country Town, and when I called again, she was full of eagerness to say, 'Why, sir, that Cranford is all about Knutsford! My old mistress, Miss Harker, is mentioned in it ; and our poor cow, she did go to the field in a large flannel waistcoat because she had burned herself in a lime pit !'"

214

BETAKE yourself, in these new days, to Omar Khayyám ; and what he sings of the fleeting joys of life and the consoling grape, say you of summer. For the long hours will weave themselves into ropes of sand you may not hold, and the brown leaf-stems loosen on the trees ; the earth will by-and-by lock up her treasure-box, now jealously opened, and you must shrink back into winter hiding, owning that the feast was spread and you kept a foolish fast, that summer stayed at your hand and you craved no guerdon. Throw aside therefore the fevered craving to read books and to rouse the world's wonder over your haste. Set the mind only upon flowing water and bountiful trees, and that in no studious mood, but the warm languor of a midday dream. And note well that an upland pasture is good hunting for the soul, and so also is the moving sea ; but you shall mar the spell of their spirit upon you if you creep under roofs

by night. For that is a sickly fashion,
born of fear and a crowded life; and it
constrains the soul. Form a happy company of such as love the earth, and set
up your tents by sea or lake, or even on
the hilly pasture slopes at home. And
this adoption of the outer world shall
make a reason, not for carousing and re-
enacting the sports of winter, to offend
the face of heaven, but it shall serve as
withdrawal into the sanctuary of true
repose. There shall be long hours spent
"in a green shade;" still, serene float-
ing on the lake, while the sunset burns
to gold, and deep dream-locked sleep
under canvas or in the open air. I
would not forbid you to read Stevenson
and Lanier, but the modern novel shall
be held afar from your rest. Your muscles shall ache with tramping and the
oars; you shall be bruised from stum-
bling through the forest when you steal
out by night to feel the dark among the
pines; you shall find the simplest fare
ambrosial; and you shall be called to
life, every morning, by a chiming chorus
and the hoarse logic of the legislating
crows, and wake to see, oh, matchless
wonder! the ferns and raspberry vines

breathing outside your tent and painting the shadow of their trembling on the sunlit walls. Easy is it in England to suffer a summer change into vagrom ways, tramping the blossomy lanes, eating under hedges, and begging the kindly carrier for a lift in his van ; and even in America two women, comrades pledged, may forswear roofs and walk abroad with staff and scrip, or even set up their tent in a huckleberry pasture, near some farmer, lord of New England soil. None so necessary as he ; for he shall be the purveyor to their comfort, and give them milk and eggs for the dirty bills born of winter's drudgery, and turned now to something worthy through righteous use. The camper, to civilized minds, entertains a bee in her bonnet, in that she loves her dripping house by the wood better than timbered roofs, though Solomon had raised them. Her bee drones happily, and all the little world hears it ; but its very presence invests her with a certain sacredness, like that of madmen in days of old, and the farmer-folk are her leal protectors from hunger and the world. These be the tamer ways of camping, and pleasant withal ; but if

four or more strong spirits can betake
them to the deeper wood where even
the sound of mowing and garnering invade not, and make their summer home
by lake or stream, they shall seize hold
of the garment of their youth even
though she were vanishing away. They
shall work hard, and love it. They shall
cut a path to the strip of beach where
the water is clear over sand and beguiling to the bather ; they shall row miles
for the potatoes for to-morrow's dinner,
and tug mightily to pile up the sticks
for next day's fire. Fighting thus the
old battle over again, warring to fill the
simpler needs of life at first hand, is
to return with gladness to our great
Mother, and cling about her knees. The
ancient struggle for life shall be enacted
in little on their sunny stage ; and they
shall see the earth more clearly, as
through the eyes of old, and think, too,
on the stars, nearer now in that they
brood and smile. Certain pitiful falla-
cies shall be unlearned through the
lessoning of camp. The wise pupil,
stultified by civilized theory, finds with
amazement that no more secure and
solemn retreat exists than the forest

path at night, and that darkness is as little to be feared as her own cloak. She grows into the acquiescence of animals under a summer rain ; nay, even to joy therein, and gains an added lightness when the sun breaks forth. A pillow is no longer the mainstay of sleep, and she dozes excellent well on a bed of pine needles with an arm tucked under her head. And, oh, the feasting of the eye! line upon line of trembling branches, enthralling shadows of leaf on sunlit leaf! The remembrance of it, to one who has had that rich surfeit, is like a song in the heart. Perhaps that is what the thrush sings in forest aisles, when twilight falls : the shapes of things, the form and color, all the glorified remembrance of his golden day. Who shall say no ? For after all, what but a thrush's song could trace upon the mind's fine tablet the outline of a leaf ?

This it is to be fortunate at home ; but he who crosses the sea earns a double blessing : and if he go to tramp, to gypsy, he has found out what it is to gather up the gold of the year and garner it away for winter spending. To walk is truly to live. When the morning

shines before you and with it a broad
highway, stretching straight into bliss,
you may throw up your heels at fate.
But there are roads and roads; some of
them lie in the mind forever, in lines of
light. One such is the way out of Brecon to Llansaintfraed, where the bones
of Henry Vaughan have long been crying from a neglected grave: another is
the Roman road out of good Shrewsbury,
and a third the broad highway whereby, after Monmouth, you go on to the
beauties of Tintern and the Severn Sea.
There they wait for you, conscientious in
milestones, relics of a conquering past,
and some of them beguilingly setting
forth the number of miles from London;
thereby, no matter what your loyalty to
green fields and beneficent sky, drawing
the heart out of your breast with longing. Your only companioning there
shall be the infrequent farmer's wain,
the wandering tinker and the unmistakable genus tramp, sometimes pursuing
his slouching way, but oftener asleep on
his face under a hedge. But fear him
not. He is our cousin, and the comrade-
ship of wandering is strong between us.

You shall learn strange things of the

English churl and what serves him for mind, while you invade his roads and valleys. It will not be long before you formulate the axiom that he knows not one hand from t' other; for when he sends you to the right, it is well established out of the mouths of many witnesses that he honestly means the left. You must never ask him a question on a sudden, for haste addles his wits, and he will swear he knows not Joseph. Two of us, one day, after manifold disappointments in such queries, which served only to lock up the knowledge indubitably there, arranged a set of questions which might have proved of unfailing excellence had time and the hour given a margin for their use. For instead of the crass query, "Can you tell me the way to Babine?" we would invent a cunning preamble, thus: "Good morning, goodman. A fine day! It is very pleasant walking. We hope to get on to the next village. We do not know it by name. We think it may be Babine. Pray you, what *is* the name of the next village?" Thus delicately jogged, Master Shepherd's wits might of themselves leave their wool-gathering, and he would send us on equipped. But jarred too rudely, denial seems his only refuge.

" Is this Tretower? " I asked a rustic one day when that heaven lay palpably before us.

" No, miss," he responded.

" Is n't that Tretower? "

" No, miss."

I turned away, adrift, but with one last impulse varied the phrase.

" What is that village? "

" Tretower." He had recovered.

And when such are awakened to the point of directing you, they do it by a system calculated to induce madness in the natural mind.

" You see that church? " begins your informant.

" Yes." Naturally you make a mental note of the church.

" Well, *go you by that.* You see that woman walking? "

" Yes." You speak hastily, for meantime she is in motion. You begin to see what life must have been for Alice, playing croquet when the wickets would walk about the ground.

" There the road turns. But go straight on. Yours will be the next one." And so by indirection, a certain negative process, you learn what you must not do, and come, by slow and painful steps, to what you may.

"Turn up on your right hand at the next turning, but at the next turning of all, on your left; marry, at the very next turning, turn of no hand, but turn down indirectly to the Jew's house."

Here have we historic precedent.

And ever, having finished some complicated direction, they conclude in triumph: "You carn't miss it!" To some of us who have missed it many times, even while the echo of that prophecy died upon the air, it is a terrifying phrase. I have grown to consider it the equivalent of the evil eye.

The good walker eats lightly in the middle of the day. Save at happy moments of active good fellowship, he talks little. His feet settle into the rhythm of the road, and his mind reposes on the happy continuance of measured effort. He never thinks. He is conscious only of ecstatic being, or the richer state of an acquiescent content. He has learned what it must be to fly like the pigeon, to live under water, to

take root in the earth and grow. How
effortless life may become they only
know who have tasted the joys of the
road. Here are pretty paradoxes. The
feel of the pack is no burden, but an
added gift ; but so, too, is the freedom
of casting it aside for the noonday rest.
One loses respect for clothes in the
main, yet conceives a tender liking for
some benignant article like a pair of
ragged gaiters, a dress too impossible
to be spoiled, or an old hat gloriously
adorned with a mad - cap pheasant's
feather, found by the way. The track
is diversified like life itself. In one
summer you may learn what it is to
tread the highway, to flee over Egdon
Heath, pursued by thunder-clouds and
Dorset tragedies, to lose breath in the
hot fragrance of Devon lanes, to tramp,
knee-deep in heather, over the Exmoor
hills, or scour Salisbury Plain, thyme-
scented, loud with larks.

What the byways of wandering may
be only he can guess who searches in
the corners of his mind for rich treasure-
trove cast in there on fortunate days.
Certain walks of our own lay placidly
along canals, — Brecon, Llantisilio, or

even the water way to Iffley along the
Thames.   There was one upward range,
on Haughmond Abbey day, when we
came on great patches of brilliant
sward, under black-boled beeches, making their own green shade.   Still above
lay drifts of wild hyacinth, "like blue
peat smoke against the sky."   We
remember lengths of Welsh road, again
azured by hyacinths and cool yellow
with primroses, where the clearest of
streams run swiftly, so that you seem
to be moving in their good company;
and you dip your dusty feet therein for
comfort and for benison.   Sometimes
entertainment falls richly on you expect-
ing nothing; at a mansion torn by Par-
liamentary cannon-balls, or a farmhouse
like one near the Battlefield of Shrewsbury, where nature's gentleman gave
two of us to drink of milk foaming in
newness, and then led us in to see his
carven mantels and wainscoting that
were old when the Lords of the Marches
kept their state.

The world and the glory thereof are
yours, and every night you swing into
town or hamlet, eat dreamily but with
mighty appetite, and betake yourself to

sleep, wherein you seem to be walking, still walking. For the muscles themselves retain the rhythm of motion, the while they rest. The best legacy of all is perennial, even after the prisoning walls have shut you in again. Sometimes at night you see, beneath closed eyelids, two silent figures swinging along on a summer road. These are you and your good comrade, though indeed they do not seem to be you at all, but two far more happy than imagination could guess. They are walking, always walking, and the sun shines and speedwell thrives under the hedge; they smile as they go. Sometimes, in a foolish play, they divert themselves hours long by snapping the bags of bladder-campion, ambitious only in that rivalry. They are children, rich in their changing foothold of earth and mothered by the sky. They are not you: yet the sight of them brims over with peace and promise, and you go smiling away to sleep.